Six Nights in Paradise

ASHLEY CADE

Ashley Cade

Book cover design by Cassy Roop / Pink Ink Designs
Formatting by J.M. Walker / Just Write Creations
Professionally edited by Stacy Sanford / The Girl with
the Red Pen
Proofreading by Tiffany Hernandez

ISBN: 9780578717944

Also by Ashley Cade

Wild Hearts Series
Something That Could Last
Everything We Left Unsaid

Playlist

Six Nights in Paradise Playlist
"Rock The Boat" by Aaliyah
"Drunk On A Plane" by Dierks Bentley
"Temperature" by Sean Paul
"No Letting Go" by Wayne Wonder
"Hips Don't Lie" by Shakira ft. Wyclef Jean
"Turn Me On" by Kevin Lyttle
"Somewhere On A Beach" by Dierks Bentley
"Sangria" by Blake Shelton

Prologue

Taylor

THIS IS IT. IT'S FINALLY *happening.*

I leaned against the driver's side door of his hand-me-down Tahoe. It was a faded hunter green with cracked leather seats and the permanent stench of fast food and pizza clinging to the interior, but I didn't care. It was *his* car. I'd ridden in it at least a hundred times, but never just the two of us. Tonight was going to be different. Tonight I would make him mine.

I'd finally gotten up the courage to approach him and tell him how I felt. He would be graduating in less than four months, so this was my last chance.

I waited for him to emerge from the gym. He'd sunk the winning shot in the final game before playoffs started and was most likely just now showering after a long and raucous celebration with his teammates. I could be patient. I'd been waiting for this moment for three years, ever since I realized I was madly in love with him. I had a plan, and nothing was going to stop me from executing it tonight, not even if I had to wait hours for him to come out of the locker room.

When the side door finally opened, I straightened my stance and wrapped my arms around my body, portraying the abandoned little sister left out in the cold. My expression morphed into one of innocence, belying my sinful intentions.

He waved goodbye to someone still inside and walked toward his waiting vehicle, a relaxed smile playing on his lips as he watched his feet. When his gaze lifted and he caught sight of me, his smile fell away and his expression turned serious.

"Taylor, what are you doing out here? It's freezing." He picked up his pace, his long legs eating up the distance between us quickly. His hands came up to frame my arms, rubbing up and down to warm them. I felt the heat of his touch, even through the layers of stuffing in my winter coat.

"I missed my ride," I said, letting my eyes drift to the ground, pretending to be embarrassed. "I saw your car still here and was hoping you could take me home."

"Yeah, of course. Get in," he instructed, unlocking the doors. I slid into the passenger seat as he fired up the engine.

"Why didn't you call somebody?" he asked, a hint of scolding in his tone. I hated when people treated me like this, like I was some kind of child. He was only three years older than me. I let it slide, though. I didn't think there was anything I couldn't forgive him for, and he seemed so genuinely concerned. "It's way too cold to be waiting out here."

"Phone's dead." I shrugged, the lie falling easily from my lips.

"Oh." He cranked up the heat and pulled out of the parking lot, heading toward my house, the streetlights casting their soft glow over the black top.

"Can you just," I began with a sigh, "not take me home yet?"

He glanced over at me and worry creased his brow. "Why not? Is something wrong?"

"I'm just not ready to go home." It wasn't a lie, but wasn't quite the truth, either.

"Where do you want to go?" he asked in confusion, glancing at the clock on his dash. It was getting late and my curfew was quickly approaching. I had less than an hour to execute my plan. I was running out of time and needed to make my move.

I bit my bottom lip, suddenly nervous. What if he rejected me? What if I'd been imagining all those looks he'd thrown my way, the seemingly accidental touches when he brushed by me in the kitchen or the media room?

I took a deep breath, preparing myself. It was now or never.

"How about Hunter's Point?"

He slammed on the brakes so hard, my body jutted forward, the seat belt scraping the side of my neck as his SUV skidded to a stop. His eyes flashed to mine and I sucked in a breath. Hunter's Point was *the* make out spot for kids at our high school. Asking him to take me there made my intentions perfectly clear.

After a few intense seconds, he shook himself and looked away, easing his foot down on the gas pedal. He drove in silence for a moment before pulling off into an abandoned parking lot. Shifting into park, he gripped the steering wheel with both hands and stared out the window, his shoulders and jaw tense. Finally, he returned his gaze to me and shifted in his seat, angling his body toward mine. I unbuckled my seatbelt and leaned across the center console.

"Taylor, we can't do that." He looked pained when he said it, as though he didn't really mean it and it hurt him to lie to me.

"Why not?" I asked, my voice low and seductive. At least that was how it sounded to my ears.

"You're Aiden's baby sister. He'd kill me if I so much as kissed you." His eyes fell to my lips and I licked them. The action was involuntary and subconscious, but exactly the right move. His eyes flared with heat and he sucked in a breath. Before he could stop me, my mouth was on his. I kissed him, pressing my hands against his chest. His heartbeat skyrocketed under the hard planes of his pectoral muscles.

And he kissed me back.

I opened my mouth and his tongue slipped inside. He tasted like Gatorade and cinnamon gum, and oh, what a delicious taste it was. We lost ourselves in the moment and I reveled in the feel of him, of the soft pressure of his lips against mine.

Finally.

Suddenly his hands were on my shoulders, pushing me away. Our mouths broke apart and he stared down at me, his breath coming in and out in rapid little bursts like he'd run out of air. He turned from me and ran his fingers through his hair in frustration.

"Damn it," he cursed, slapping his hands against the steering wheel. "Don't do that again," he demanded without looking at me.

"What?" I cried. How could he say that? We were having a moment. We finally kissed and I was ready to make him mine. To become his.

"I don't think of you like that," he declared and then winced.

What the hell?

"But," I began, fighting back tears, "you kissed me," I said, touching my fingers softly to my lips, trying to capture the feel of his kiss and commit it to memory.

"No," he bit out. "*You* kissed *me*."

Why was he so mad about it? He seemed to like it just fine a minute ago. Now he was acting like it was a mistake.

He regretted kissing me. And there I was, preparing to offer up my virginity to the boy I'd been crushing on since seventh grade.

My face flamed with mortification. *He doesn't want me. He never wanted me. How could I be so stupid?*

"Take me home," I demanded with a sniffle. Tears slipped down my cheeks and I turned away from him, staring out the window pointedly.

He reached for my hand, whispering my name, but I jerked it away as soon as I felt his touch.

"Just take me home," I repeated.

He sighed and shifted into gear. The short drive home felt like an eternity, the quiet discomfort a suffocating third wheel nestled between us. I regained my composure and dried my eyes, hoping no one would notice I'd been crying. When he finally pulled into my driveway, I got out before he could say anything and bolted to the door. I fumbled with my keys, my hands shaking, the sound of blood rushing in my ears. A hand on my forearm startled me and I dropped them, the bundle of metal landing with a dull thud on our welcome mat. He bent to pick them up and slid the pink key marked *Home* into the lock, opening the door to my salvation. Before I could get away, his hand landed on my arm again, his grip gentle, apologetic. I looked up into his pained eyes and my heart cracked open a little.

"Please don't tell your brother about this," he pleaded, a hint of fear tightening his features. I frowned, not expecting that to be the last thing he said to me tonight.

"Don't worry," I assured him. "I'm not going to tell *anybody* about this." He hung his head and scrubbed a hand over his face, his eyes full of regret. Before he could say anything else, I stepped inside and shut the door, shutting him out entirely.

We never spoke of the incident, pretending it never happened. But he came over less and less, most likely to avoid running into me. When he was there, I found a reason not to be. When he left for college, I breathed a sigh of relief, glad not to have to face him, or what I thought was the biggest blunder of my romantic life.

Turned out, I was capable of far worse.

One

DALTON

"I CAN'T BELIEVE SHE called off the wedding with only five days to go!" Aiden fumed from the corner of the island, both hands braced against the marble, his jaw clamped tight as he shook his head.

My eyes remained locked on the counter, varying hues of grey, silver, and white swirling over the speckled surface. I let the tranquil pattern lull me into a false sense of peace. I should've been fuming, too. "At least she didn't leave me standing at the altar," I mumbled before taking a swig of my beer. "Silver lining, I guess," I offered with a shrug, still in shock from the bomb my fiancé – well, *ex* fiancé now – dropped on me two nights ago.

Gianna and I had been engaged for nearly two years. Our wedding was supposed to go off without a hitch this weekend. She and her mother had planned everything down to the last detail. The caterer was booked and had been paid months ago. Our venue was the most sought-after wedding destination in the city. We'd secured our date and paid our deposit as soon as I slipped that ring on her finger. The wait list was a mile long, and if we hadn't secured our spot that very moment, we would've missed out on the prime date during peak wedding season. Thank God her parents were footing the bill for everything else except the honeymoon, because it put a serious dent in my savings, but I was more than willing to do whatever made her happy.

Too bad it wasn't enough.

"How can you be so calm about this?" Aiden asked incredulously. "She called off your fucking wedding!" he nearly shouted. "After everything was paid for! You're never getting that money back!"

I brought my hand to my face, pinching my brows together before scrubbing my fingers over my stubble-covered jaw. I hadn't shaved since that night, the night my world came crashing down on me.

Two nights ago

"I can't do it, Dalton," Gianna announced from across the table. We were at Exeter having dinner before everything became so hectic that we wouldn't have time to share a nice meal together until the rehearsal dinner.

"Can't do what, babe?" I asked before placing the bite of steak I had just sliced away into my mouth and chewing.

"I can't marry you."

My jaw froze mid bite and my gaze settled on hers. She wrung the napkin in her hands furiously, her lips pulled into a regretful frown.

I forced down the inadequately chewed morsel and set my fork on the plate. "I'm sorry," I croaked, shaking my head. Surely I hadn't heard her correctly. "What was that?"

"I'm calling off the wedding. I don't want to get married."

A warm, metallic taste filled my mouth as I took in her distressed expression. I realized finally, when my cheek began to sting, that I'd bitten down so hard on the inside of it that I'd drawn blood.

"Don't you think that would've been important to tell me months ago?" I asked, my shock swiftly turning to fury. "You know, before I spent *thousands* of dollars to give you your dream wedding and honeymoon?" I threw my napkin down, my appetite suddenly gone.

"I'm sorry," she whined. "I didn't want to hurt you."

"Don't you think *this* is hurting me?" My anger turned to panic as the pain of what she'd said finally started to seep into my chest. "Gianna, we're getting married in less than a week. If you're getting cold feet, we can talk about it. We'll get through this."

"Were," she replied.

"What?"

"We *were* getting married," she corrected. "I didn't want to do this to you, but I've met someone else."

The rage returned, hot and insistent, ready to boil over the edge. I flexed my jaw and covered my mouth with my hand. I wanted to yell at her, to shake some sense into her, but I couldn't. She had me at a disadvantage. We were in public and the last thing I wanted was to cause a scene. She'd planned this out well.

"Who is he?" I asked between gritted teeth, ready to commit murder.

"That's not important."

"The hell it isn't!" My voice rose, drawing the attention of diners at other tables.

"Keep your voice down," she hissed.

"How can you expect me to stay calm when you've just told me you have a side piece and you're cancelling our wedding – which, by the way, is only five days from now – because of *him*?"

"He's not a side piece," she said, her mouth tightening in irritation. "We have a real connection."

Was this really happening? Was my fiancé really throwing away the last three and a half years of our lives together to be with someone she *had a real connection with*? What. The. Fuck.

"Look Dalton, things have been going downhill between us for a long time now," she began, and I frowned. *What the hell is she talking about?* Our relationship was great. "Antonio makes me feel special. He makes me feel like you used to. I think I need to give what's blossoming between us a chance."

I'd heard enough. I couldn't listen to another word of this nonsense. Scooting my chair back, I stood and pulled several bills from my wallet, tossing them down on the table. I didn't know who this woman was, but she wasn't *my* Gianna, that much was clear.

"You're making a big mistake," I told her calmly; not threatening, not warning, just informing. She would regret this. She'd always been impulsive, but never with anything as important or life changing as this. Maybe if she took a day to think on it and got a good night's rest, things would be clearer for her in the morning.

But they weren't clearer. Less than twenty-four hours after breaking off our engagement, she moved Antonio into her condo and all that was left of her memories with me were packed in a cardboard box and sent to my office.

What was supposed to be the happiest week of my life turned into a living nightmare.

"What am I supposed to do? I already lost my shit," I confessed, shame filling my chest. "There's currently a hole the size of my fist in the drywall next to my bathroom mirror." Aiden's eyes widened and snapped to my face. *Ugh, why did I just admit that?*

"Totally understandable, man. Sometimes you just gotta let the demons out," he offered in understanding. "She's been keeping some other guy's dick wet. I'm surprised you didn't rip the sink off the wall."

I scowled as the rage I felt that night started to creep back in. My fists balled at my side and my jaw clenched so tight, I thought my teeth might grind into dust. I thought I was over it. I thought I'd yelled, punched, and cussed my way past her betrayal, but hearing someone else say what she did out loud brought the pain and devastating anger back to the surface. I threw back my beer, chugging it all in one go before slamming the bottle back onto the counter. I was fuming, and not even an ice-cold beer could cool the flames. Aiden took in the tight set of my jaw, my rigid posture, and brooding countenance.

"Sorry, man," he apologized. "That was insensitive."

"It was the truth," I ground out. "And I needed to hear it." I needed to come to terms with what she'd done. She cheated on me. While I was planning our forever, anticipating the moment I'd watch her walk down the aisle in a long white dress, she was off screwing some guy who couldn't even manage to wear matching socks. That's right. I went to her condo to see what she'd thrown away our chance at happiness for and saw him with his too-long hair, mismatched socks, and paint splattered tee shirt. He was an "artist," she claimed. He looked like a hipster trying to find a sugar mama to fund his cannabis farm.

"What are you going to do with your plane tickets and reservation at the resort?"

His question brought me back to the present. That was actually my whole purpose for being there.

"Well, they're non-refundable, so unless I want to cut my losses, I have to find somebody to take her place and go with me." I looked at him pointedly, hoping he'd get the hint.

"Oh, no," he began, straightening and holding his hands up. "Don't look at me. There's no way I can leave right now."

"Oh, come on, man. You're my best friend! We're both single. We'll be in another country. There will be beautiful women running around in bikinis and plenty of rum to keep us nice and comfy."

"Dude, no. I'm up for a big promotion and we have not one, but two major clients to meet with next week. If I spring a last-minute vacation on them now, I can kiss that promotion goodbye."

Shit. "What about Travis?" I asked hopefully, going down the line of our closest friends.

"He's studying for the bar exam. No way he's going to take off right now."

"Shawn?" I questioned, the hope starting to drain out of me.

"Bethany will kill him. She only has a month left before the baby gets here, and she's already having contractions. He's not even allowed to leave the county right now, much less the country."

I pulled out my wild card. It was my last resort. "Well, does Adam have anything going on?"

"He's in rehab," Aiden deadpanned. "Again. He can't even leave the center for a couple more weeks. It's court-ordered this time," he added sadly. I winced, hating myself for not knowing he had relapsed again. What kind of friend was I?

A shitty one.

Seemed like I couldn't do anything right these days. I lost my fiancé to another man and couldn't even be bothered to keep up with the four guys who had been like brothers to me.

Two

Two weeks ago

WHY DID I ANSWER my phone? When I saw it was the university calling, I should've just let it go to voicemail. I wasn't ready to deal with this. I wasn't ready to face the consequences of my actions. I'd been misguided and naïve, and now I was paying for it.

My hands wrung together, my foot tapping a fast-paced beat against the hardwood floor as I waited in the sturdy wooden chair outside the dean's office. This was it. I was about to get kicked out of school. What was I going to tell my parents? I'd have to think of something convincing, something so far from the truth that they'd never guess what I really did.

While I was getting ready this morning, I did my best to look innocent, even though I was far from it. I had to convince them I belonged there, that I didn't do anything wrong, although nothing could be further from the truth. What I did was *very* wrong, and I knew it. This morning, I dressed in conservative clothes, ensuring my skirt wasn't too snug or short and there was no cleavage showing. I applied minimal makeup, allowing the slight smattering of freckles across my cheeks and nose to shine through when I usually concealed them, and opted to wear glasses instead of putting my contacts in. I looked demure, non-threatening, inculpable. I needed them to believe me incapable of what I'd been accused.

My heart leapt into my throat when I heard the door open and watched the dean emerge. "Hold my calls," he instructed his secretary, and then his gaze slid to me. "Ms. Wesley," he greeted. His tone was indifferent, professional. He wasn't thrilled to have me in his office, but he didn't outwardly show his disdain. I was confident this wasn't the first time he'd had this conversation with a student, and it probably wouldn't be the last.

I stood from my chair and grabbed my purse, my hairline and underarms dampening with nervous perspiration. I suddenly regretted the sweater set I'd slipped into, hoping it gave me the look of a dedicated and rule-abiding college student. It was far too warm for the knit material and long sleeves. At least my skirt was knee length and didn't cover my legs entirely. I'd mercifully left the panty hose off as well.

Mr. Crawford motioned for me to follow him and I did, smoothing a sweaty hand over my clothes. "Have a seat," he instructed, pointing to the chair across from his desk. Another man I recognized but couldn't place was perched in the seat next to his desk. From the placement of my chair, I guessed that his chair had been next to mine, but he moved it away. They wanted to show a united front, to draw a line between us. Them on one side and me on the other.

"Ms. Wesley," Mr. Crawford repeated after settling behind his massive, ornately designed desk, "there have been some serious accusations made against you. Accusations of this nature require thorough investigation, and your cooperation would be greatly appreciated."

I swallowed hard, willing myself to keep my mouth shut until he was done speaking. I wanted to lie through my teeth and shout my confession all at the same time. If I could've lied, just denied the whole thing, this might have gone easier. But I'd learned years ago that lying never got me anything except hurt, so I vowed never to do it again.

My heart raced as he read over a list of the things that had been reported to him about me. I gripped the arms of my chair, my fingernails biting into the soft leather. When he finished, he removed his reading glasses and set them atop the papers in front of him.

"Now," he began, folding his hands together, "what do you have to say about these accusations?"

My mind screamed to me, *Deny! Deny! Deny!* I wanted to. I wanted to make this all go away, to go back in time and make a different choice. But nothing could erase what I'd done. No amount of pleading or begging would make it go away. So, I folded and told the truth. I told them everything.

Three

"**I HAVE NO IDEA** what I'm going to do." I raked my hands through my already messy hair and hung my head. "There's nobody else I can take. I guess I'll just have to go by myself."

"Do you really think that's a good idea?" Aiden asked, one eyebrow raised skeptically. "I foresee you doing a whole lot of drinking while you're there, and you're going to be surrounded by water. I'd hate to see you get smashed, fall into the ocean, and end up drowning yourself."

"How do you even come up with this shit?"

He shrugged and took another swig of his beer. "Just trying to think ahead, bro."

I shook my head, contemplating his concerns. I supposed his points were valid. I did plan on drinking myself into oblivion for the next week. The location and company were irrelevant. And if I was lucky, I'd fuck Gianna out of my memory.

Speaking of drinking myself into oblivion... I popped the top off another beer and glanced up, catching sight of Aiden's sister, Taylor entering the kitchen. Both Aiden and Taylor still lived at home with their parents. Taylor was still in college and Aiden was saving up to buy a house. There really wasn't any reason for either of them to move out. The house was huge, so nobody felt crowded or like anyone was constantly in their business. Their parents let them come and go as they pleased as long as they cleaned up after themselves and didn't have rowdy parties. My mom had never been anywhere near as laid back as Mr. and Mrs. Wesley.

Taylor froze when she saw me, and a little stab of pain pierced my chest. She didn't care much for me, hadn't for many years. And that was all my fault.

"Hey, Taylor," I greeted, my eyes tracking her movements.

"Hey," she offered in a small voice. She seemed a little down, even more sullen than usual. But she was still so beautiful, with her black rimmed glasses perched on her small, slightly upturned nose and her hair pulled into a messy bun sitting atop her head with a few wispy tendrils snaking along her bare neck. I cleared my throat and averted my gaze, ashamed I could think about my best friend's baby sister that way. He would cut my balls off if he knew all the sordid things I'd fantasized about doing with her.

Ever since the summer after she turned fourteen and wore a bikini for the first time, I was a goner. I'd never paid her much mind before that, always placing her in the category of annoying little sister just like Aiden did. But that day, when she stepped out onto the back patio in her pink bikini, I looked at her as a woman for the first time. She'd developed over the winter, her long, baggy sweatshirts and leggings hiding what her swimsuit put on full display. Aiden caught me staring and punched me in the arm.

"You lay a finger on her and I'll cut off your dick," he warned and I winced, rubbing the spot he'd hit.

"What?" I feigned innocence, pretending like I hadn't just been ogling her.

"Dude, I'm not stupid. You're getting a boner checking out my little sister," he accused, glancing toward my crotch. Sure enough, he was right. I covered myself with my hands and turned my back to her so she wouldn't see I was already flying at half-mast. "Sicko," Aiden sneered quietly enough that only I could hear.

After that, I tried my damnedest to ignore my attraction to her, afraid of what her brother would do to me. But it never faded away. Over the years it only grew stronger, and several times I had to remind myself I was taken. Gianna was gorgeous, an absolute stunner. But I still found myself searching Taylor out at social gatherings and birthday parties, even though I had no intention of ever stepping out on my relationship with Gianna. Too bad she hadn't extended me the same courtesy.

I shook myself from the memory as Aiden grabbed us both another beer from the fridge, sneaking a look at Taylor as she opened the pantry door. Her shirt rose as she raised up on her tiptoes to reach for the jar of Nutella on the top shelf. My eyes glided down her torso and over the exposed skin of her lower back before settling on her ass. I swallowed hard and looked away just in time. Aiden turned back to me and walked over to where I remained standing at the island. He tilted his head to the side and looked over at Taylor as she grabbed a spoon and twisted the lid off the jar in her hands. He looked back at me before returning his gaze to his sister. When his focus landed on me again with a mischievous glint in his eyes, I started to panic.

No. He's not going to suggest…

"Why don't you take Taylor?"

Taylor's gaze snapped to his, the spoon full of Nutella halted halfway to her mouth.

"What?" I asked incredulously.

"You need someone to use the other ticket, and Taylor," he began motioning to her, "isn't doing anything else right now." My brow furrowed and I looked at her.

"I thought you were in school?"

Aiden rolled his eyes. "She's taking a break right now." His tone suggested judgement and disapproval and I bristled a little. Taylor's face fell and she dropped the spoon back into the jar, her appetite lost.

"It makes perfect sense," he continued, oblivious to the pain his little barb caused. She'd quit working when her studies became too intense to keep her grades up and hold a job, and Aiden never passed up a chance to remind her that he had managed both. What he failed to mention was that he could study at work, while she never had that luxury. "She has no other obligations holding her back, and you need somebody to take Gianna's place on your trip."

Taylor stiffened, her eyes going wide with recognition. "I don't think so," Taylor announced as I whispered a soft "no."

"I can't go, and neither can any of the other guys. Who else are you going to find on such short notice?"

My eyes drifted back and forth between the two of them. Taylor looked slightly panicked, while Aiden's smug face just oozed satisfaction. He thought he was so fucking smart coming up with this solution. *If he only knew.*

"I," Taylor stuttered, "I'm supposed to look for a job," she countered.

"It's only a week. You can look for a job when you get back," Aiden said. "It's an all-expenses paid vacation to a luxury, five-star resort," Aiden explained. "In the Caribbean," he added for effect. He knew how much she loved the beach and was baiting her. "I think the time away will do you some good."

Her gaze settled on me and I hated how timid she looked. That wasn't her. She was usually bold and outgoing. She was looking at me, searching for some sign of how I felt about the situation, but suddenly I couldn't speak. The thought of being in a tropical paradise with Taylor, with her taking my fiancé's place, would either be an absolute disaster or the sweetest form of torture. I'd get to see her body scantily clad in itsy bitsy bikinis every day but wouldn't be able to touch her. We'd be forced to remain in the same space with each other longer than we had been in years. The scent of her body wash would linger in the air after her shower, and I'd be forced to sit there while she was only a few feet away, naked and wet.

"Did you even ask Dalton if *he* was okay with you asking *me* to go on *his* trip?"

Aiden gave her an exasperated look and turned to face me. "Are you okay with Taylor using the other ticket, that will go to waste, otherwise," he began, flashing a pointed look back at his sister, "and taking this trip with you?"

What the hell was I supposed to say? I looked back and forth between the siblings, my best friend and his little sister that I'd tried my hardest not to be attracted to for the last eight years. I really had no other option. None of my friends could go. My mom couldn't get the time off work on such short notice. Trust me, I realized how weird it was to ask her, but if anybody deserved a free vacation, it was her. So, unless I wanted to take this trip solo, which felt really pathetic, Taylor was my only option.

"Sure," I resigned with a shrug. I didn't want to seem too excited about it, even though the thought of seeing Taylor in a bathing suit was already making me hard. Thank God the island shielded my groin from her view. I turned my body slightly, angling it away from Aiden, just in case. "Can you be packed and ready to go Sunday morning?" Gianna and I had planned on catching an early flight so we'd have most of the day to enjoy the sand and surf, hoping we wouldn't be too exhausted from the festivities the night before.

"Yeah," she replied sheepishly. "I can do that. What time should I be at the airport?"

"I'll pick you up at six. We can ride together." There was no point in both of us driving and paying to park two cars. It just made sense to pick her up. Her shocked expression confused me and it took me a moment to realize what caused it. We hadn't been in a vehicle together since that night. The night she kissed me after my basketball game and I had to push her away, pretending it wasn't exactly what I'd been dreaming of for over a year.

"See? It's all settled then!" Aiden announced, clapping me on the back. "Aren't you glad I'm such a great problem solver?"

Little did he know that what he just did was guaranteed to create far more problems than it solved.

Four

I **WAS SO NERVOUS,** I hardly slept a wink Saturday night. I tossed and turned, imagining all kinds of crazy scenarios that would never happen. Like Dalton finally noticing me and looking at me as more than just Aiden's little sister. Him kissing me, touching me, pulling the strings of my barely-there bikini and watching it fall to the ground. Wishful thinking, huh?

I didn't know how I'd make it through this trip with him. How could I pretend for six long days and nights that I wasn't completely enamored with him? How was I going to sleep under the same roof with him and resist the urge to sneak a peek while he changed clothes and disrobed for his shower? This would be pure torture.

I had my bags packed and waiting by the front door the night before, so all I needed to do this morning was get myself ready. My stomach fluttered in anticipation as I waited for Dalton's car to pull into the driveway. At five minutes past six, I saw headlights shine through the windows of the front room, casting their yellow glow along the back wall.

He's here! I'm really doing this. I was going to spend the next week with my adolescent crush, taking the place beside him where his new bride was supposed to be.

My heart broke for him. Regardless of how I felt about Gianna, Dalton loved her. Personally, I found her to be snooty and aloof, always looking down her nose at me. Literally. She was five-foot-ten, a whole four inches taller than me. With rich, dark brown hair, startling blue eyes, and curves for days, she was a total bombshell. I could see why Dalton fell for her. I just couldn't see why he stayed once the shine wore off. Don't get me wrong – she was still drop-dead gorgeous, but her personality was seriously lacking. She'd been groomed to find a suitable match, one her elitist parents would approve of. She had a degree I was certain her father paid for, in more ways than one, that she never used. All she did was shop and post on Instagram. She was a socialite and nothing more.

Dalton, on the other hand, scraped and fought to get where he was. He grew up the only child to a single mom. His deadbeat dad hit the road shortly after he was born, claiming he wasn't cut out for fatherhood. Dalton watched his mother work her fingers to the bone just to keep the lights on and put food on the table.

When Dalton was offered a scholarship to play ball out of state, he jumped at the opportunity. Even with his mother in a better position financially after obtaining her own degree, he was determined to do everything on his own. Now, he was the senior director of product development for a major Fortune five-hundred company. He'd climbed the corporate ladder at blazing speed. He was smart and knew how to think outside the box. If he kept going at that pace, he'd be a senior VP before he hit thirty.

My pulse quickened when the phone in my hand buzzed, the screen lighting up with a text from Dalton. We'd exchanged numbers that day in the kitchen to ensure ease of communication regarding this trip. I didn't want to read too much into it, but fifteen-year-old me had damn near jumped for joy.

I grabbed my bags, locked the door behind me, and headed to his shiny black Lexus. Dalton had money. He was a young, successful businessman and could afford nice things. I couldn't imagine how much it cost to book his honeymoon. Probably as much as my tuition for the year. No wonder he didn't want to let it go to waste, but now I felt bad for not paying my own way. Not that I had much money of my own, but my parents were well-off. They could compensate him for my ticket and share of the hotel or condo where we'd be staying.

"Hey," he greeted me breathlessly after hefting my luggage into the trunk. I may have gone a little overboard packing for a trip where I probably wouldn't be wearing much more than a bikini with the occasional sundress, shorts, and tank thrown in. "You ready?" A shiver ran down my spine, thinking about how little we'd both be wearing all week. It was gonna be hot where we were going and therefore, a lot of skin would be exposed. Despite my nerves, I was looking forward to that part.

"Yeah, I can't wait!"

A smile tugged at the corner of his lips. "Me neither."

The fluttering returned to my belly and I pursed my lips together to avoid smiling like a fool.

The drive to the airport was quiet, the air between us slightly charged. A ball of nerves tightened in my stomach and I wrapped my arms around my waist in an attempt to ease the tension. The last time I'd ridden in a car with Dalton I threw myself at him, then tucked my tail between my legs when he rejected my advances. I hoped he'd forgotten all about that. Maybe he'd experienced enough cringe-worthy moments with other girls since then that my blunder wasn't even a blip on his radar anymore.

He switched on the radio and I was instantly relieved for a break in the silence. The volume was low and I could barely make out the song. When I realized what was playing, my breath hitched and I sat up a little straighter in my seat. Aaliyah's "Rock the Boat" drifted softly from the speakers, its sensual lyrics and accompaniment weaving its way between and around us like a tether that would bind our hearts together forever. This was no way to start our completely platonic tropical getaway. This song was too sexy, too suggestive for us. I fought the urge to reach down and switch the station since it wasn't my car.

Dalton cleared his throat and shifted in his seat. My gaze swung to his face, taking him in. He looked just as uncomfortable as I felt. "How about something more current?" he proposed, reaching for the controls.

"Sure," I agreed a little too quickly. He let out a soft chuckle and switched the station. I relaxed back into my seat, watching the sky begin to lighten as we neared the airport.

"Can I get you something to drink?" the flight attendant asked, flashing a blindingly white smile at Dalton. Our first-class seats were ridiculously comfortable. Takeoff was going to feel much smoother from this end of the plane.

"I'll have a Jack and Coke," he replied.

"Dalton?" His name was out of my mouth before I could stop it. *How the hell could he drink this early in the day?* He turned an inquisitive look at me, one eyebrow quirked. "It's not even nine in the morning," I informed him in a low voice, my tone more reproachful than I intended. His jaw ticked and his look turned into a glare. I'd just said the wrong thing.

"Well, seeing as it's my honeymoon, I plan on drinking throughout most of the next week."

"It's your honeymoon? Congratulations!" the attendant gushed, looking back and forth between us. Uh oh. This wasn't going to be pretty.

"Actually, Naomi," Dalton began, studying her name tag for a second before settling his stony gaze back on her face, "congratulations aren't really in order. You see, my fiancé called off our wedding six days ago, and I couldn't get a refund for this trip." Her eyes widened and she opened her mouth to speak, but he kept going. "I'm heading to what was *supposed* to be my honeymoon with my best friend's little sister, because she's the only person in my life not doing anything else this week."

His comment stung. It wasn't like I didn't know that was the only reason I was there, but until that moment, I still had hope that he would actually enjoy my company. Now the truth was perfectly clear. He was only tolerating me because he didn't want to take this trip alone.

"I am so sorry," she began, but he held up a hand.

"I'll take that Jack and Coke now," he demanded. "Do you want anything?" His question was directed at me, but his eyes weren't. He refused to look in my direction. He was brooding, his posture rigid and jaw tense.

I wanted to reach out and comfort him, maybe apologize for overstepping, but I knew better. The flight attendant's congratulations opened a wound that had finally started to heal, and even though his words hurt, I tried not to hold it against him. He was supposed to be *married* right now. Gianna, his beautiful bride, should've been in the seat I was occupying. Instead, he was stuck with me. I vowed in that moment to give him his space. I'd make myself scarce as soon as we landed and let him lick his wounds in private. He didn't need me there watching him, quietly observing as he put the pieces of his broken heart back together.

"Just a water, please," I answered sheepishly, my voice low and remorseful.

Three tumblers of double shot Jack and Cokes later, Dalton was feeling much better. I tried to convince him to eat something to soak up all the alcohol, but he refused. He was getting wasted and there was nothing I could do about it. The attendant brought another drink and he tossed it back quickly. The more relaxed he became, the friendlier he was towards her. Once she realized he and I weren't really a couple, she started flirting with him hardcore. If this had been a movie, Dierks Bentley's "Drunk on a Plane" would've been the accompanying soundtrack. He was getting smashed, and by the seductive look Naomi was giving him, he was dangerously close to joining the Mile-High Club.

I shrank back into my seat and stared out the window, unwilling to witness their exchanges any longer. Resting my head against the cool glass, I closed my eyes, willing this flight to be over as soon as possible.

I awoke sometime later to the sound of Dalton lightly snoring next to me. We both fell asleep at some point, and boy, was that a mercy. I yawned and stretched my muscles, wondering how long I'd been asleep. I glanced over at Dalton's watch, surprised to see I'd slept most of the flight. We would be landing within the hour. Dalton stirred next to me but didn't wake. I decided to let him sleep this one off, and hoped he woke up sober and in a better mood.

Five

DALTON

I WAS JOSTLED AWAKE when the plane's tires hit the runway, the aircraft bouncing as it lost momentum and rolled to a stop. Taylor was curled into herself, staring out the window. I watched her for a moment, not wanting to disturb her. She looked so tiny and withdrawn. Regret burned like bile in my throat. I was nasty to her and she didn't deserve it. I'd bristled at her judgement and lashed out. She was probably right. I shouldn't have been drinking that early in the morning, and now I had a headache because of it.

"Taylor," I began, and she swung her gaze to me. She unfurled her limbs and sat up in her seat. "Look, I-"

The overhead speakers crackled to life and our captain's voice drowned out my apology as he announced we'd reached our destination. She stood and collected her things before I could finish, and I suspected she knew what I wanted to say. I rose from my seat and took a few stumbling steps, following behind her. I was apparently still a little tipsy. Not a surprise, considering how much I drank.

I'd slammed back a couple more after Taylor fell asleep, and when my bladder could no longer wait to be relieved, I snuck off to the tiny bathroom. Naomi was waiting for me when I slid open the door. She pushed her way inside and pressed her body against me. Her lips met mine and her hands tangled in my hair. I let myself get lost in her, opening my mouth and sliding my tongue over her lower lips, dipping it inside as she moaned. After several minutes of making out, my body naturally reacting to her attentions, she offered to blow me, right then and there. She didn't know how good that sounded. I desperately needed the release. So why did I hesitate? Gianna was no longer in the picture. I was a single man, free to do whatever I wanted with whomever I wanted. But something held me back.

Taylor's face flashed into my memory. I worried that she would somehow know what I'd done if I chose to let this stranger pleasure me, and for some reason, that gave me pause. I gently turned Naomi's offer down and returned to my seat, quickly passing out from a cocktail of whiskey and exhaustion.

We stepped out into the bright Caribbean sun and I brought my hand to my face, shielding my eyes. *Ugh, Taylor was right. I shouldn't have drunk so damn much.*

We took the shuttle to our resort, sitting quietly next to each other on the bench seat. When the doors finally opened, she stepped out behind me and gasped. The private villa was even more breathtaking in person.

"*This* is where we're staying for the next week?" I nodded. "Holy shit!" she exclaimed in wonder.

I unlocked the door and pushed it open, stepping into the large, open space. We dropped our luggage just inside the door and began exploring. I checked out the living room with its massive flat screen, wondering who the hell would want to watch TV in a place like this, while Taylor went to the kitchenette. I gravitated to one of only two closed doors and twisted the knob, seeing that it led to the bedroom.

My face fell and I let out a low curse when I saw the bed. It was covered in rose petals with towels shaped into a heart resting in the center. I never thought to notify them that this was no longer going to be my honeymoon, and all these extra touches were unnecessary. I stood there, frozen as Taylor chattered away in the hall. I knew the moment she entered the room, her sharp intake of breath echoing in the large space.

"Dalton," she said, her voice laced with compassion as she gently laid a hand on my upper arm.

Her touch sent a little zing up my arm and through my body. The pain of Gianna's betrayal was slowly fading, but my desire for Taylor was growing. What would she do if I kissed her right now, threw her onto the bed that I'd intended to share with someone else, and explored her luscious body with my mouth? I looked into her big doe eyes with their burst of green just around the irises that faded into a muted hazel. She had no idea what she was doing to me, and I needed to keep it that way.

I stepped out of her reach and walked to the sliding doors across from the bed. They opened onto a shaded patio that housed an outdoor tub and looked out over a stretch of private beach just beyond. White sand disappeared into turquoise water that sparkled like diamonds under the sunlight. This place was paradise.

"I'll take the couch in the living room," I informed her, keeping my gaze locked on the ocean. I was afraid if I looked at her, she'd see just how badly I wanted her. The two of us hooking up was a terrible idea for multiple reasons. For one, I wanted my genitalia to remain intact and I valued my life. I didn't want to face Aiden's wrath if he found out I'd defiled his sister. Two, I didn't want to use her to get over Gianna. She deserved better than to be somebody's rebound. I wasn't in the best state of mind right now and couldn't offer any emotional stability. It would be best if I just kept my distance.

"Don't be silly," she scolded. "This is *your* vacation." I appreciated that she refrained from using the proper term to explain what this was meant to be. "And I just crashed it. You take the bed and I'll sleep on the couch."

"No way," I countered, finally turning to face her. "I'm not letting you sleep on the couch. My mama raised me better than that."

She straightened her spine, digging her heels in. It took all my strength not to let my eyes settle on her perky breasts and the lacy bralette peeking out from under her flowy tank and stay focused on her face. I could tell she was gearing up to be really fucking stubborn and it was turning me on.

"I'm not letting you sleep on the couch. *You* paid for all of this. *You* deserve the bed. Besides, you're too tall for the couch."

Shit, she had a point. Still, I couldn't do it. I couldn't make her sleep on the couch while I luxuriated in the plush, California king-sized bed with its one thousand thread count Egyptian cotton sheets. My mother would kill me.

"None of that matters. I would never make a girl sleep on the couch when there's a perfectly good bed available."

"Alright," she began with a challenging tone, her eyes narrowed on me, "how about this?" Now I was in for it. "We're both adults. We can share the bed." My eyes widened in surprise and I had to clamp my mouth shut so it didn't fall open. Was she really suggesting we sleep together? In the literal sense? "This bed is huge," she continued, motioning toward it with her hand. "I'll take one side, you take the other."

I swallowed back my rebuttal. I couldn't tell her that having her in my bed, platonic relationship or not, would be far too much temptation for me. I couldn't tell her that things would most definitely go too far if she was within arm's reach. Outside of those facts, I didn't have a valid argument to make. We *were* both adults. We should be mature enough to share this giant ass bed without making a big deal about it, but I didn't know if I was strong enough for that.

"Okay," I found myself saying. I was probably going to regret this. By the time the week was over, my balls would be the color of a smurf's. "If you can live with that, so can I."

"Deal," she announced, reaching out her hand. I took it and tried to ignore how soft and warm her palm felt against mine. Our eyes locked and the satisfied look fell from her face. I held onto her a second longer than necessary and something vulnerable and carnal flashed in her eyes. I knew if I didn't let go, things would quickly get out of hand, so I released her and stepped back, clearing my throat.

"Do you want to get unpacked?"

"I was actually thinking about getting my bathing suit and hitting the beach." She stared longingly out the expanse of windows lining the back wall of the bedroom. We still had a few hours of daylight left, so there was plenty of time to enjoy the sand and sun.

"Sounds like a great idea. Mind if I join you?"

"Not at all."

I hauled both of our suitcases into the room and we dug out our swimwear. She slipped into the bathroom to change and I quickly threw off my clothes and stepped into my board shorts. She came back wearing a flimsy, sheer, white cover-up over her floral bikini. I never understood why girls bothered with those. You could practically see right through them, a fact I wasn't hating at the moment.

We made our way down to the water and I was pleased to see a couple of beach chairs already set up. The villas on this side of the island were spaced far enough apart to afford us a little privacy, so there wasn't anybody else near our little section of beach. The sand was powdery soft under our feet and the water was just cool enough to be refreshing. We waded in waist deep and I fought the urge to reach for her. Instead, I headed in the opposite direction and dove under the water to cool my rapidly heating skin. I didn't know if I was so hot because of the tropical sun, or as the result of Taylor's close proximity.

After about an hour, we decided to head inside and get ready for dinner. I'd made reservations at one of the resort's premier restaurants and couldn't wait to dig into a pound of freshly caught crab legs. We took turns using the shower before Taylor commandeered the bathroom to get ready. She came out forty-five minutes later looking absolutely stunning.

Her light brown hair that faded into a dark honey blond at the tips fell around her shoulders in soft curls. Her makeup was light and natural, a hint of her freckles showing through. Bronzed skin, pink, pouty lips, and long, black lashes rounded out the look. Her simple cotton dress, a light yellow that made her skin tone pop, hugged her waist, accentuating her shapely hips and firm, round breasts. One thin spaghetti strap slipped off her shoulder, and I watched with rapt attention as she slid it back into place. She was exquisite.

I was in so much trouble.

Six

Taylor

I STUDIED MY MENU, trying to ignore the gorgeous man sitting across the table from me. He was dressed in khaki shorts and an aqua blue polo. It was simple, but he made it look like a million bucks.

Why did this feel like a date? Maybe it was because he slipped and told me how beautiful I looked when I came out of the bathroom. Or because he pulled out my chair, his fingers brushing over my bare shoulder and arm as he stepped around the table to take his own seat. Or perhaps it was the bottle of wine he'd requested that now sat perched in an ice bucket on our table.

Dalton laid his menu down and reached for the bottle of Sangria, pouring us each a glass. I grabbed mine and started sipping on it right away. I was tense. For the past eight years, I hadn't been alone with this man, and now I'd spent the last thirteen hours with him. His mere presence had me on edge.

Once we ordered our food and the waiter took away our menus, I could no longer hide from him. I'd been using that menu as a shield and now it was gone, leaving me feeling exposed and vulnerable. I'd planned on giving him his space, but he hadn't let me get far away from him since we arrived. He followed me out onto the beach when I tried to give him his space, and then he insisted we retain his reservation here.

I fiddled with my napkin-wrapped silverware as we waited on our appetizer. I had no idea what to say to him. We had nothing in common besides Aiden, and I really didn't want to talk about my brother. I prayed he didn't ask about school. I wasn't ready to talk about that and doubted I ever would be. Gianna was a subject neither of us wanted to broach. So, I settled for the safe option.

"How's work?" His eyes lit up a bit and my shoulders sagged with relief.

"Work's great. We're looking at some more environmentally friendly alternatives to several of our products. It took me a while to convince the team to invest in the research, but they're finally coming around," he beamed. "Consumers are becoming increasingly concerned with the environment and reducing waste. It only made sense to move us in that direction."

My smile grew as he spoke. I loved it when a man was passionate about what he did for a living, when it wasn't just a job. I'd thought that was how Jason worked, but it turned out he was only passionate about getting into my pants.

My smile fell and I shook that thought away. I wouldn't think about him right now. I refused to let him ruin my evening or this trip.

The waiter returned and set a small plate in front of each of us. A steaming hot dish of crab-stuffed mushrooms was placed in the center of the table, and a serving spoon was dipped inside. Once we both had a mushroom on our plates and the waiter retreated, conversation resumed.

"How about you? You mentioned needing to find a job."

"I was planning on working this summer. I'd like to save up so I can get my own place after I graduate."

"Don't you usually take classes during the summer?"

I tried to hide my wince at his mention of school. If he noticed a change in my demeanor, he didn't let on.

"I'm just burnt out right now." That wasn't a lie; there was just a lot more to the story. "I needed a break. I'm close to graduating, so I don't necessarily have to take any classes this time around." I'd planned on graduating early, having enough credits to secure my degree by the end of fall semester. But now, with a university-mandated hiatus, I wouldn't be graduating until next summer.

"Where were you thinking about applying?"

"I have a stack of applications," I groaned. "Probably one of the upscale restaurants downtown. My friend Aubrey works at Exeter and makes really great tips, so I thought I'd try that route." He flinched when I mentioned Exeter, but the look passed quickly. What was that about?

"Have you considered entering the corporate world? My company is always looking for interns."

"I don't know. Maybe." I shrugged. The truth was that I wasn't sure I was ready for something like that yet. I saw the strain on Aiden's face when things weren't going as planned. He'd stayed up into the early hours of the morning working on spreadsheets and proposals on more than one occasion. Waitressing was safe. It was hard, exhausting work and you had to deal with some real assholes, but at least when you went home, you could leave it all behind. It didn't follow you into your personal space.

We settled into silence, enjoying our meals. When my glass ran dry, Dalton offered to refill it and I let him. It was a sweet gesture, but I had to remind myself this was temporary. We weren't an item. This wasn't a date. This was just two friends – no, not even friends, two acquaintances– who'd both been thrown into shitty situations, trying to find solace in each other's company. When we returned home, everything would go back to normal. The only difference was, maybe now we wouldn't have to try so hard to avoid each other.

When we left the restaurant after a delicious seafood dinner, we walked back to the villa along the beach. I took off my sandals and wiggled my toes into the cool sand. Dalton got too close to the water and the small waves splashed up onto his feet, soaking the soles of his brown leather thongs. He removed them and we continued along the moonlit beach barefoot. It shouldn't have felt romantic. We weren't two lovers walking hand-in-hand along the beach under a darkened sky full of stars, but I wanted to be.

We were both exhausted from our flight and decided to turn in for the night. I let my gaze travel over Dalton's bare back when he removed his shirt for bed. *Dear Lord, he sleeps shirtless?* I noticed his skin was tinged pink and I frowned.

"It looks like you got a little burnt today." He twisted around, trying to see his shoulders. He pressed a finger to his skin and it blanched.

"Huh, guess I did," he agreed. "We were only out there for an hour or so."

"We're a lot closer to the equator down here so it doesn't take as long. How does mine look?" I turned my back to him and swept my hair over my shoulder so he could examine my skin. I could hear his sharp intake of air even from across the room and quickly realized my mistake. He padded over to me, the soft thud of his bare feet audible in the otherwise silent room. Goosebumps pebbled my arms as he brushed a few stray pieces of hair I'd missed over my shoulder.

"Looks okay to me." His voice was low and full of gravel. "How did you manage not to get burnt when I did?"

I kept my back to him, unable to look him in the eye. I knew he'd see the desire in mine, and I wasn't interested in being rejected by the same guy twice. "I've already been out in the sun quite a bit this year. I have a pretty decent base tan," I explained, hoping he couldn't hear the shaking in my voice. He was standing right behind me and his close proximity was doing funny things to my insides. "We'd both better wear sunscreen tomorrow."

"Yeah," he agreed absently.

"I have some aloe gel in my bag if you'd like to use it," I offered once he finally stepped away and the scent of his skin wasn't invading my nose and subsequently turning my brain to mush.

"Thanks. That would be great."

I retrieved the big bottle of blue goo and handed it to Dalton. He applied it to his shoulders and the top of his back, but kept missing a deepening pink area between his shoulder blades.

"Here, you missed a spot." I held out my hand, requesting the bottle back. He turned and looked at me quizzically before passing it to me. I squirted a little onto my fingers and pressed them to the tender skin. He hissed from the cold gel, but it warmed quickly from the heat radiating off his body. I reveled in the sensation of his smooth skin under my hands, the muscles of his toned back flexing and stretching. I wanted to keep touching him, but I had no reason to. His entire back was coated and now it was time to let it absorb. I reluctantly pulled my hand away and took a step back.

"There," I announced with finality. "Should be all better by tomorrow."

"Thank you." His soft, appreciative eyes landed on me and I gulped. His torso was perfection. He was all hard slabs of carved muscle. His abs flexed as I raked my gaze over them before locking on the grey sweatpants settled low on his hips. My mouth watered and I yearned to run my tongue over every deep-cut ridge of his stomach.

"No problem," I mumbled absently. His soft chuckle pulled me from my perusal of his body and my face flamed. He caught me. I was totally just checking him out and I got busted. *Shit.* "I'm gonna get changed for bed," I said quickly, grabbing my clothes and escaping to the restroom. I washed my face and brushed my teeth before slipping on my yoga shorts and my brother's decade-old debate team tee shirt. It was several sizes too big, the cotton extra soft from years of wear and multiple washes, making it more comfortable than any pajamas I'd ever owned.

I slipped under the covers quickly upon my return to the bedroom. Dalton had turned out all the lights except for the lamp on his bedside table. He was reading something, but set it down when I came in. He walked silently to the bathroom, returning a few minutes later. He switched off the lamp and slid into bed.

"Goodnight, Taylor." The minty scent of toothpaste wafted across the bed and I licked my lips, wishing it was his lips instead of mine.

"Goodnight," I whispered and pulled the covers up to my chin. I could do this. I was a mature adult sharing a room with another mature adult. He didn't think of me like that, so I had nothing to worry about. *Yeah, right.*

A warm hand slid beneath the loose material of my shirt and splayed across my stomach. My synapses fired to life and my eyes sprung open. I was still in the villa and there was a hot, hard body pressed against my back. *Dalton.* I squeezed my eyes shut, willing myself to wake up from this dream. There was no way this was really happening, and I didn't want it to go too far because I'd just be disappointed when I awoke.

He groaned and dug his erection into me, the hard ridge pressing against the soft globe of my ass. A soft moan fell from my lips and I couldn't decide if I wanted him to slide his hand higher or lower. He made the decision for me. His fingers brushed the underside of my breast and I bit down on my lip to keep from making too much noise. He buried his nose in my hair and kissed my neck, his hand coming up to fully cup my breast. He squeezed and rolled the nipple between his thumb and forefinger and I arched into his touch.

"Dalton," the whisper fell from my lips and he froze. He didn't move for several seconds. Then he cursed and scrambled away from me like he'd been burned. like I was made from lava. I sat up on my elbows, watching him in confusion.

"Shit, Taylor. I'm so sorry!"

What?!

"I was dreaming," he blurted out frantically. "I didn't realize it was you."

My heart sank. He'd been dreaming of someone else, probably his ex-fiancé, while he was touching me. I sat up all the way as he jumped out of bed, pulling frustrated hands through his hair. He was distraught. He was distraught because he felt me up and ground his rock-hard cock against my body, imagining I was someone else. An ache settled into my chest. He would never see me as anything other than Aiden's little sister. Nothing about me did anything for him. I would never be good enough to garner his attention.

I got out of bed, intent on escaping to the bathroom before the tears began to fall, but Dalton's voice stopped me. He came up behind me and placed his hands on my arms. I fought back the urge to throw them off and storm out.

"I didn't mean to do that. I really am sorry."

I took a deep breath, regained my composure, and turned to him. "Not a big deal," I assured him falsely. "It happens." I shrugged and turned my back on him, finally escaping to the bathroom.

When I emerged, Dalton was in the kitchen slicing up fresh mangoes and pineapple for breakfast. I eyed the white bag resting on the counter that wasn't there last night.

"What's that?" At the sound of my voice, his head shot up and he immediately looked apologetic. I wanted to slap that look off his face. It was a reminder that I could never have him.

"I ran out to the little cafe we passed on the way in and grabbed some pastries." I hadn't realized I'd been holed up in the bathroom that long. I lost track of time standing in the shower, letting the hot water pour over me in an attempt to loosen my tightly wound muscles.

He placed several chunks of fruit on two plates and added a danish to each. We sat on the covered patio facing the ocean and ate our breakfast in silence. Maybe now that I knew without a doubt where I stood with him, firmly in the friendzone, I could stop feeling so tense around him. I just had to keep telling myself that.

Seven

I **AM AN IDIOT.**
Why did I think I could share a bed with Taylor and *not* have my hands all over her? Her body felt fucking amazing. Her skin was smooth as silk and smelled like vanilla. Her breasts were full and heavy, her body responsive and needy when I touched her. I haven't seen her nipples, but I could tell how perfect they were just from feeling them.

"Fuck," I grumbled to myself as I leaned my head against the shower wall, the hot water stinging the already tender skin on my back. I didn't know if I could share that bed with her again. We had five nights left. Five more nights of painful restraint and torture. What would happen tomorrow morning? Would I slide my hands down instead of up next time? Would my fingers slip inside her panties and find her wet and ready? Shit, I had to stop thinking about her like that. She was going to catch me with a hard-on I wouldn't be able to explain away. Next time, I wouldn't be able to lie and make her believe I was dreaming about someone else.

Taylor was already in the ocean when I returned to the bedroom. She was wading around, skimming her hands over the water, with her face tilted toward the sun. I took a moment to just watch her. She looked so serene, her honeyed hair hanging down her back and dipping into the water. She wore a coral bikini this time, the bright color accentuating her deepening tan. I knew from years of experience that her freckles would become more prominent the more bronzed her skin became. I wanted to join her, but I already had a slight sunburn and didn't have any sunblock. I turned to head for the kitchen and caught sight of a tall, bright yellow can. Taylor had left her spray-on sunscreen sitting on her nightstand. I figured it was still pretty early in the day and since the sun hadn't reached its peak, I could go out this morning as long as I liberally coated myself with the white mist. Just for good measure, I threw on a light-colored tee shirt to give my back and shoulders extra protection.

Sunscreen in hand, I gathered up a couple beach towels and headed out the sliding doors. It took Taylor several minutes to realize I had joined her, but she immediately got out of the water when she saw me.

"Hey," she greeted breathlessly, wringing the saltwater from her hair.

"Hey. Did you need this?" I held up her sunscreen and she shook her head.

"I put some on already. I should be good for a little while longer. How's your back?"

"Still a little pink," I admitted. "I'm not going to stay out here long, and I'll keep my shirt on while I'm in the sun." Her lips pulled into a pout, aggrieved at my refusal to bare my torso, and I grinned. That shouldn't have made me so happy.

"Okay." She plopped down into the beach lounger. "I'm just going to read my book for a bit while I soak up some sun."

I settled into the chair next to her, taking in the scenery as I tried to relax. This place was beautiful. Crystal blue waters, lush palm trees, stuccoed villas with roofs that mimicked the tops of straw huts. It was stunning. I tried my best to look at everything but Taylor. As gorgeous as our surroundings were, none of it could hold a candle to her.

It wasn't long before the heat started to become unbearable, so I stood and walked to the water. I spent several minutes in the shallows, enjoying the coolness of the waves lapping around my hips before saying "screw it" and submerging my whole body. I came back up and rubbed my hands over my face and scalp before shaking the excess water from my hair. The dip was refreshing and the wet material clinging to my body helped cool me down. I looked up as my feet hit the dry sand and my step nearly faltered. Taylor was staring at me with her lips slightly parted and one hand pressed lightly against her chest, just under her throat. She looked at me like I was a tall glass of water and she was a woman dying of thirst.

She quickly shook herself from her reverie and picked her book back up. Her cheeks were red, and I couldn't tell if it was from the temperature or from embarrassment. "You look hot."

Her head snapped up. "What?" she gasped, and I almost felt bad for the double meaning.

"Your face is red. You should get back in the water and cool down," I instructed.

"Oh," she replied, tucking a damp strand of hair behind her ear. "Yeah, I probably should." She wedged her bookmark between the pages she'd been pretending to read and left the paperback in her seat. I stayed until she'd had enough of the water and returned, her face back to its normal shade.

"It's starting to get really hot. I'm going to head back in for now."

"Okay."

I went inside, changed out of my wet clothes, and hung them in the bathroom to dry. Settling in with my laptop, I was determined to get a little work done while I was cooped up inside.

Fifteen minutes later, I was knee-deep in my response to a colleague's email when movement from outside the window caught my eye. I lifted my gaze. Taylor stood and adjusted her beach chair so it was nearly flat. Hesitantly, she glanced from side to side and I sat up a little straighter. What was she looking for? There was no one around. She was alone on our little private section of beach. When she reached behind her back and started to pull the strings to her bikini top, I realized what she was about to do. She was going to sunbathe topless.

Holy shit.

The strings gave way easily and she moved to the ties behind her neck. I cursed, sat my laptop aside, and walked to the door, prepared to stop her. But what would I say? She'd be bare by the time I got to her. I wouldn't be able to focus on anything but those luscious breasts, the rosy tips pulling into tight peaks from the breeze off the ocean.

I couldn't just walk out there and demand she cover up, could I? It wasn't my place, but I knew Aiden would want me to do something. He'd want me to protect her and keep her in line. Then again, she was a grown woman who could make her own decisions. No one had the right to tell her what to do. So I waited, wavering between inaction and instinct.

Her top dropped to the seat I'd recently vacated and she settled back into hers. Her head was raised just enough that I couldn't see anything, and I felt like a fucking creep for trying to. I turned away, unwilling to be the type of guy who peeped at a half-naked girl without her knowledge. Returning to my abandoned computer, I attempted to focus on my work, my eyes frequently searching her out, ensuring she was still there. God help me if she ventured off somewhere. I would have to go after her then.

Several minutes later, I looked up to find a small group of guys, three college aged punks, walking toward her on the beach. They were looking at her, elbowing each other and smiling, their greedy eyes roaming lustily over her form, and I sprang into action. Before I could make it to the door, she must've noticed them too, because she sat up and grabbed her beach towel, haphazardly spreading it across her chest in her haste.

No one heard me open the door over the sound of the waves, and they didn't notice me as I approached. I came within earshot just in time to hear one of them taunt, "Come on, girl, show us what you got. You can't pretend to be shy now that you've gone topless."

"I didn't think anybody else was out here."

Her voice shook with timidity and I felt my blood begin to boil. They were scaring her. Enraged, I picked up my pace, reaching her chair in seconds. All three of the guys froze when they saw me.

"Is there a problem here?" I gritted out through clenched teeth, purposefully lowering my voice an octave.

"No sir," one of them replied.

"We were just admiring your girl's," another one chimed in, pausing to think of the right word, "assets," he continued with a smirk, clearly not recognizing the danger he and his friends were about to encounter if they didn't back off. His buddy elbowed him and rubbed his thumb over his nose nervously. When I took a step toward them, my fists balled and ready to strike, they took a step back.

"I suggest you continue your walk and keep your hands and eyes off her *assets*," I warned. They scampered off without another word and I turned my glare at Taylor. It wasn't her fault those kids were horny, disrespectful little punks, but *shit*. If she didn't want anyone to see her tits, she should've kept her top on.

"Thank you," she said quietly and stood, grabbing her things before bolting inside. I turned to watch her leave and noticed her reflection in the window. You couldn't really see inside, and I realized she never would have noticed me watching her. God, I *am* a creep.

Eight

MY FACE HEATED, CHEEKS burning with embarrassment as I scurried past Dalton to escape back inside. Those guys saw me. They saw my naked breasts and leered at me. Who knew what they would have done if Dalton hadn't come to my rescue?

Dalton.

He was the only person I thought might see me topless. I'd actually hoped he would, and subsequently liked what he saw. Maybe then he would touch me on purpose next time. Maybe then he would caress my body without dreaming I was someone else. It was a pathetic, last-ditch effort to garner his attention and hopefully win him over.

Boy, did *that* plan backfire.

Escaping into the en-suite, I let my head fall against the back of the door. I needed to get it together and chase any thoughts of Dalton and I hooking up while we were here out of my head. It wasn't going to happen. He would never see me as anything more than his best friend's little sister.

I splashed cold water on my face and finger-combed my hair. It actually looked pretty good, the saltwater giving the soft waves a little texture. It looked beachy and effortless and I loved it.

When I exited the bathroom, Dalton was perched on the corner of our bed waiting for me. *Our bed.* A shiver ran down my spine at that thought. We were sharing a bed for the next five nights. Too bad nothing fun would be happening there.

His eyes found mine when he heard the door click shut and I stopped dead in my tracks. He was brooding, his eyes flaring with anger.

"What the fuck, Taylor?" He rose and faced me, his jaw tight with annoyance.

"What?" I asked, stunned by his tone and language. He'd never spoken to me like that before.

"What were you thinking, going around topless like that?"

My mouth curved into a frown. The hope that he'd finally notice me dissipated, replaced with defiance and retaliation.

"I wasn't 'going around topless'," I snapped back. "I was sunbathing and decided I didn't want any tan lines." That was only partially true, but he didn't need to know the rest. He didn't need to know I was banking on him seeing me and liking what he saw. "Besides, there was no one around. I didn't think anybody would see me," I added, hating that I felt the need to explain myself to him.

What about me? Didn't you consider that *I* would see you?" he challenged.

Consider it? Hell, I'd prayed for it.

"What would it matter?" I challenged right back. "It's not like you would've looked." I was baiting him, waiting for him to break. Waiting for him to admit something, anything. That he wanted to see me, that he secretly snuck a peek at me through the glass, hoping to see what my bikini kept hidden.

His chest rose and fell with his deep inhale and his jaw ticked again, his eyes dropping briefly to my chest.

"Your brother would kill us both if he found out I let you go out there exposed like that." He motioned toward the beach, completely avoiding my question.

"What do you mean, if you *let* me? You have no say in what I do. I'm an adult and you're not my dad, so it's not really up to you what I do or how I choose to dress." I glared at him, the passion of my lust quickly morphing into anger.

His shoulders slumped in defeat and he scrubbed a hand over his face. "I didn't mean it like that," he offered apologetically, his tone softer. "It's just," he paused, searching for the right words, "I promised your brother I would keep you safe. He's trusting me to make sure nothing happens to you. I take that trust very seriously." His tone was so sincere, his eyes pleading, that it cooled my rising temper. "I'm sorry," he added.

Suddenly, I was overcome with remorse. I overreacted, allowing the feelings I'd harbored for him to cause me to behave irrationally.

"It's fine," I muttered, brushing past him. "I should've known our little stretch of beach wouldn't remain empty all week." And that thought made me a little sad. I wanted him all to myself. I would've been just fine seeing nobody but him on this island for our entire stay. But I knew he didn't return those sentiments.

Several hours later we were dressed for the evening, dinner reservations he'd booked months ago awaiting us at one of the resort's five-star restaurants. I tried not to let it bother me that he'd planned on taking his new wife to dinner, not me, but it caused something deep inside my chest to ache. He wasn't mine, and up until a week ago, he belonged to someone else entirely.

Dalton informed me that the place we were heading this evening was a bit more formal than where we dined last night, so I slipped on the only cocktail dress I brought with me. It was a snug little black number that hugged my hips and waist, pushing my breasts as high as they could go. The thin spaghetti straps framed my cleavage, flattering my modest C cups and drawing his eyes to the enticing swells of my breasts. I wasn't extremely well endowed in the bust department, but in this dress, you'd never know it. Dalton swallowed hard, his Adam's apple bobbing noticeably when I finally turned to face him. I'd needed his help zipping up my dress, and he did so with only a little hesitation. I could feel his hot breath against the bare skin between my shoulders as he slowly slid the zipper up, his hands lingering on the material a second longer than necessary. Or maybe that was just wishful thinking, my mind playing tricks on me.

He stepped back and averted his gaze, guilt and shame washing over his features. The moment before, he looked at me as though he wanted to tear the dress from my body and feast on *me* instead. Maybe that was my imagination, too.

He cleared his throat before speaking. "Ready?"

I nodded and slipped on my shoes before grabbing my clutch and heading out. The sun was still a couple hours away from setting, but the breeze off the ocean made the tropical temperature more bearable. We walked to the restaurant and were ushered to our table right away. Dalton's eyes found mine immediately after settling into our seats, his intense gaze searing into me. I couldn't get a read on him. One minute he looked like he wanted to rip my clothes off, and the next he watched me like one would an overcurious toddler, with disquieted apprehension and a healthy fear of the inevitable.

We sat in awkward silence as our waitress poured us each a glass of champagne, boasting about how it was authentic, flown in directly from the Champagne region in France. I gulped down my first glass quickly, trying to ease my nerves. I was flustered. A palpable tension had settled around me and Dalton, and I couldn't guess what had caused it. He sat stiffly in his chair across the table from me, uneasiness pulsating off him in waves. Things were changing between us, and I didn't know if it was for the better.

I refilled my glass as Dalton sipped at his own and perused the menu. Once we ordered, the champagne and conversation flowed more freely and he began to loosen up. Our dinner was phenomenal, even better than the previous night. I drank a little too much, so I was a bit stumbly as we exited onto the street. Neither of us was ready to return to our villa, so we decided to explore more of the island. We hadn't seen much of it yet and were ready to remedy that.

Now that the sun was beginning to set, the resort was coming to life and had transformed into an island-wide party. Music and laughter spilled onto the streets, as well as a parade of people. The doors to the bars were flung open and live entertainment was on every corner.

Dalton scowled as a man clapping along with a street band began to dance with me, twirling me around and dipping me dramatically before slipping a tropical flower into my hair, tucking the stem behind my ear. I laughed, not only at his perturbed expression, but at how much fun it was to dance with a stranger in the street.

We stopped in front of a night club that looked promising and he tilted his head to the side in question. I nodded, ready to let loose for a bit. "Temperature" by Sean Paul pounded out of the speakers, the volume nearly deafening when we made it inside. Several people were already on the dance floor writhing and shaking their asses to the beat, half empty drinks balanced precariously in their hands.

"Want a drink?" Dalton's breath tickled the skin below my ear, causing goosebumps to spread over my arms. His body was so close to mine, his mouth nearly touching my lobe, that I had to suppress the urge to close my eyes and lean into him. I reminded myself he was only doing this to be heard over the music, not because he actually wanted to get close to me.

"Sure," I shouted back. Lightning shot up my arm when he grabbed my hand and tugged me toward the bar. He dropped it quickly once we'd maneuvered our way through the throng of tipsy club hoppers and the sensation was lost. A few minutes later, he handed me a colorful drink with a paper umbrella sticking out of it. He grabbed his cup of beer and found a couple of empty seats at one of the tables near the DJ.

I sipped my drink as the awkwardness from the beginning of the night started to seep back in. Dalton watched the crowd, doing everything he could to avoid looking at me. The longer we sat there, the more annoyed I became.

If he didn't want to hang out with me, why did we even come in here?

Draining the rest of my drink in one gulp, I slipped out of my chair and headed for the dance floor. I thought I heard Dalton call my name, but it was so loud in there, it was hard to tell for sure. I began to move, the liquor and champagne coursing through my body and loosening my limbs, my inhibitions slowly fading away.

I danced alone for several minutes, not caring about having a partner, especially if it couldn't be Dalton. Until a very tall, very good-looking man with a shaved head and perfectly unblemished dark skin stepped up to me, his appreciative eyes rolling over my body. He gave me a genuine smile before leaning in to speak into my ear.

"Could I dance with you?" he asked with a deep, slightly accented voice.

His scent permeated the air around me and I breathed him in. He smelled incredible, a clean masculine scent with just a hint of spice. And he was considerate enough to ask to dance with me, unlike most of the guys I'd encountered in clubs who liked to just come right up to you and start groping and trying to dry-hump you. This guy definitely deserved my attention. He looked like Morris Chestnut and Tyson Beckford had a love child. I wasn't about to say no to having his body in close proximity to mine. Maybe he could make me forget about Dalton for a little while, forget about the unrequited love being rubbed in my face every second of the day.

"Sure," I offered flirtatiously. He slipped an arm around my waist to bring our bodies closer and we started to move. We found a rhythm quickly, his hard body grazing mine as we danced. I couldn't help but smile. This was the most fun I'd had since arriving. Soon he was turning me and pulling me back against his chest. His hand slid around to my waist, his large palm splayed over my stomach. He felt nice pressed against my back.

But Dalton felt better.

My smile faltered with that thought and I pushed it away. This man wanted to be here with me, wanted to be in my space, moving his body against mine. I refused to let thoughts of my temporary roommate ruin this moment.

My smile fell completely when I lifted my gaze and saw Dalton staring at me, his eyes blazing with fury. He stood at the bar, his posture stiff, with a shot glass clenched in his hand. He threw the shot back, swallowing it down in one gulp before slamming the glass back down next to a second empty one and wiping his mouth with the back of his hand. He stalked toward us with his fists balled at his sides and his jaw set tight. The song currently playing came to an end and there was a brief lull as one song faded into the next. That was the moment Dalton reached us and I stopped moving.

"May I cut in?" he asked gruffly, staring straight into my eyes, though his words were seemingly aimed at my dancing partner.

"That's up to the lady," his deep voice boomed from behind me.

I turned to face him. "It's okay. I know him," I offered with a smile.

"Alright," he said, his eyes flashing to Dalton before landing back on me. "I'll see you around…"

"Taylor," I offered.

"Nico," he replied, reaching out his hand. I took it in mine, basking in the warmth and strength. He leaned in and grazed my cheek with a departing kiss before disappearing into the crowd.

I turned to glare at Dalton for interrupting my fun, but he invaded my space, pulling me into his chest before I had a chance. He began to move immediately as the music crescendoed, returning to its previous intensity. Wayne Wonder's "No Letting Go" set the tempo for our first dance of the evening. I hoped he'd listen to the words and stop holding back. I wanted him to let loose and let me in, but I doubted he ever would.

I was so in shock that he was dancing with me and that he'd permitted us to get so close, allowing so much of our bodies to touch, that at first, I didn't pay any attention to *how* he danced. But as Shakira began to croon and Wyclef spit his rhymes, I started to realize that he could really move.

Dalton James knew how to dance.

I'd never seen this side of him before. During the few high school dances I'd seen him attend, he mostly stood off to the side with the rest of the cool guys who refused to step foot onto the dance floor unless they were dragged there for a slow dance by their dates.

His body moved fluidly to the rhythm. It was sensual, especially with one leg wedged between mine and his arm wrapped around my waist. His eyes locked onto the stretchy black material sliding up my thighs as my knees bent and widened, my hips curving and swirling, and I realized he could probably see my panties. I've never been more thankful for the black lace thong barely covering my lady bits than I was at that very moment.

He lifted his head and his gaze found mine. His eyes drifted to my mouth and settled there for several seconds. *Is he going to kiss me?* Something resembling pain flashed across his face and the moment was lost.

What the hell was that?

He stepped away and turned my body much like Nico had, but I suspected it was so he didn't have to look at me, and that stung. Two seconds ago, he looked so intense and aroused; why would he turn away now?

The answer pressed into my lower back as the music changed once again, and I gasped. Kevin Lyttle's "Turn Me On" began to play as Dalton clamped one arm around my middle and clasped his other hand over mine, aligning our arms. We rolled our hips in tune with each other, our skin slickening with sweat. Aside from his accidental groping that morning, this was the closest we'd ever been, but it still wasn't close enough. I wanted him inside me. His tongue, his fingers, the hardened length pressed against my back. I wanted it all.

When the music ended, he released me and stepped back. I turned to face him, noticing how tense he looked as he ran his fingers through his hair. "Do you want another drink?" he asked, and I shook my head. I was sobering up and all I wanted was him. "Are you ready to go?" He sounded breathless, and I felt it all the way to my core.

Did I do that to him?

"Yes."

He didn't reach for my hand this time, but I still followed him. The night air chilled my overheated body as soon as we stepped outside. Dalton stormed down the street and I had to jog to catch up with him.

"Wait up!" I called and he slowed.

"Sorry," he mumbled an apology over his shoulder, continuing to plow past the crowd.

"Do you wanna talk about what happened back there?"

He finally stopped and turned to face me. "What are you talking about?"

"I'm talking about that dance." I motioned back toward the club, my tone conveying my meaning. It was more than just a dance and he knew it.

He studied me carefully for a moment, a silent war being waged in his mind. When he finally spoke, I had to fight back tears of frustration.

"It was just dancing," he claimed, his eyes skittering past me, taking in the people passing by us.

I knew better than to speak past the emotion clogging my throat. I knew my voice would crack and tears would spill down my cheeks if I tried to refute him.

"Right." I nodded my head and looked away, suddenly too exhausted and embarrassed to continue this conversation. There was no way I was imagining things this time. He was attracted to me. He wanted me. The proof was right there, poking me in the damn back. Why was he denying it? Did he feel guilty because of Gianna, because they were supposed to be married right now? She sure as hell didn't feel guilty about cheating on him. She broke off their wedding for the guy she'd been seeing behind Dalton's back.

I picked up the pace, my irritation propelling me forward. I didn't wait for Dalton. He'd find his way back easily enough. He didn't need me. *Or want me*, a tiny voice in the back of my mind chimed in.

I headed straight to the bedroom when I got back and sat on the edge of the bed to remove my shoes. My feet were aching after all that walking and dancing and I needed a long soak in the outdoor tub. Tucking my shoes away, I walked to the sliding glass doors and opened them, stepping out onto the patio. I turned the knob on the faucet and the deep, white tub began to fill with water, tendrils of steam rising into the cool night air. Walking back into the bedroom, I headed to the bathroom for a towel and washcloth, swiping my hair clip off the counter on my way back outside. I was pulling my hair up when Dalton entered the room. He didn't say a word and neither did I, but he looked frustrated. Good. So was I.

I dropped my linens on the little table next to the tub and stomped back inside to gather my toiletries, refusing to acknowledge Dalton's presence or spare him even a single glance. When I returned, I tried in vain to unzip my dress, but couldn't seem to get it past a certain point. Suddenly, Dalton's warm fingers were on mine and I froze. He'd been watching me try to remove my dress and said nothing. He remained silent as he dragged the metal puller down the length of my back, exposing my skin to the cool evening breeze. The straps fell down my arms, and I let them. I shimmied the dress over my hips, knowing he was still standing there. Now I was just being a bitch.

I turned and he cleared his throat, averting his gaze and stepping away from me. "I'll give you some privacy," he said awkwardly as he retreated inside. I pulled the curtains together, shutting him out, before removing my undergarments and slipping into the water.

When I was finished, I covered my body in coconut scented lotion and applied moisturizer to my face before dressing for bed. Dalton wasn't in our bedroom, but I could hear voices through the closed door that led to the living area. After listening for a moment, I realized it was just the TV, so I turned off the light and slipped into bed. I laid awake for a while, waiting for him to come to bed, but he never did. I finally fell asleep in the wee hours of the morning with the sickening feeling that he had stayed away on purpose.

Nine

I WOKE UP THE next morning with a kink in my neck and morning wood hard enough to act as a kickstand to keep me from rolling off the couch. Despite not having Taylor anywhere near me while I slept, I still dreamed about her. We were back in that club, dancing and grinding just like we were last night, but then everyone else faded away. We were alone on the dance floor, but this time I took advantage of that miniscule dress and tiny thong that covered very little of her.

Groaning, I sat up and wiped the sleep from my eyes. I would have to sneak into the bathroom to grab a shower without Taylor seeing me and the raging hard-on tenting my pants. Pushing the bedroom door open silently, I peeked inside. Her back was to me, but her breathing was even, so I slipped inside without making a sound and entered the bathroom, locking the door behind me. When I emerged fifteen minutes later, cleaner and much more relaxed, Taylor was yawning and stretching, her eyes fluttering open.

"Good morning," I said, and she glanced at me and muttered a groggy, "Mornin'." Then she did a double take, her bleary eyes suddenly wide and alert. I looked down my body and immediately realized my mistake. All I had to cover me was a fluffy white towel wrapped loosely around my hips, my shoulders and hair still wet from the shower. She swallowed visibly and looked away. *Shit.*

I slipped my boxers on under my towel and tried to step into my shorts while remaining covered, but it fell to the floor and I stumbled, cursing as I caught myself on the nightstand. Taylor giggled behind me and my lips spread into a grin. I knew I was being ridiculous, probably *looked* ridiculous, and suddenly the tension from the night before dissipated.

My phone chimed with an email alert and I opened it to see a reminder of the scuba diving session I'd booked for today. I checked the time and realized we needed to be there soon if we were going to keep the reservation.

"How do you feel about learning to scuba dive today?" Taylor's eyes lit up at the question and I smiled, pleased at her excitement. I'd been nervous about booking it when it was supposed to be Gianna here with me. I was afraid she wouldn't have fun or would just flat out refuse to do it. If she wasn't washing her hair, she didn't like to get it wet, and she certainly didn't like many outdoor activities or sports in general.

My smile faded as Taylor jumped out of bed and rushed around to get dressed. I was supposed to be spending this week with my new wife. We were supposed to be doing all this stuff together. Having candlelit dinners and making love every night. Going to cocktail hours and dancing together at clubs. Scuba diving and sunset cruises, and just lounging on the beach with a fruity little drink in our hands.

The ache I'd been expecting, the one that settled in my chest every time I thought of Gianna and her betrayal never came. A sadness over what we lost and all the time we wasted just for her to decide she wanted to be with someone else washed over me, but it no longer made my chest constrict like my heart was being squeezed in a vice. Maybe I was starting to get over her. Maybe we weren't even meant to be together at all. If we were, it wouldn't be this easy to move on. It wouldn't be so easy to let someone else take her place. Would it?

Taylor bounced out of the bathroom, her clothes changed and her hair braided to one side, tiny wisps fluttering around her face as she beamed at me.

"I'm ready!" she announced.

"Got your swimsuit?"

"Right here," she said, plucking a strap from under her tank top.

We packed a small bag with essentials like sunscreen and spare clothes and headed out. Taylor bounced with excited energy all the way to the training center. Since neither of us was a certified diver, we were required to take a brief course before we could go into the water. By the time we headed out on the boat, Taylor looked like she was about to burst. I almost expected her to break out into song and dance. Her excitement was palpable, and it made me glad I brought her along.

I fought the urge to reach for her hand and squeeze, knowing she would read too much into it. Our growing attraction was making it harder to keep my hands off her. The line between friendship and lovers was blurring more and more every day. She wanted me. I wanted her, but she was forbidden fruit. She always had been. Aiden was my best friend, my *oldest* friend. I couldn't put that friendship in jeopardy just to hook up with someone, even Taylor.

It seemed like no time before we were all geared up and ready to jump in the water. Taylor and I jumped off the back of the boat together, slipping under the water at the same time. We explored the hidden treasures under the blue Caribbean waters, watching as colorful fish darted by. We stayed close to each other as we neared the ocean floor, slipping past the coral reef.

Taylor suddenly grabbed my hand, pulling her body closer to mine as her eyes widened in fear. I followed her gaze to find a small shark swimming several yards away. She looked at me, the panic evident even through her goggles. I held my finger up to my lips like I was shushing her, even though I knew it wouldn't make a difference right now. It was more a warning to hold still and not make any sudden movements. She pressed in closer, scared and shaking, so I wrapped my arm around her in a comforting gesture. It felt so good, so perfect having her tucked into my side, even if her oxygen tank prevented me from pressing my hand against her smooth, toned back.

The shark finally swam away and Taylor relaxed. We floated around, navigating more reefs and schools of fish until our time was up. When we returned to land, we changed into dry clothes and went in search of something to eat, finding a casual little restaurant serving baskets of fish and chips and popcorn shrimp.

Taylor's hair lay damp around her shoulders, drying naturally in the warm air, the breeze off the ocean whipping it around her face every now and then. She tucked the unruly strands behind her ear and dipped her fries in ketchup before devouring them. We were both starving. We'd only grabbed some fruit on our way out the door this morning, in too big a hurry to stop and eat anything substantial. I pulled my phone out to check the time and noticed I had another email from the resort. Opening the app, I nearly choked on the huge piece of shrimp in my mouth. Taylor eyed me warily as I coughed and gulped down a big drink of water to clear my throat.

"What's wrong?" she asked.

"We have somewhere to be," I informed her, and she gave me a questioning look. "We're getting a massage in twenty minutes." I'd completely forgotten about booking it all those months ago. I remembered now that I'd planned this day strategically. I knew if I was going to get Gianna to agree to scuba diving, I would have to reward her with something she liked. Thus, the couples' massage was booked as her consolation prize for being a good sport. Looking back, I realized how messed up that was. But she was so damn high maintenance. It took me spending a couple days with Taylor to see just how bad Gianna had become.

We finished what little was left of our lunch and I paid the bill before heading to the address listed in the confirmation email. We made it there with only a couple minutes to spare. Leading us to a straw hut on the beach with crisp, white linen curtains opened on three sides, our massage therapists instructed us to disrobe and lie on our stomachs, offering to close the curtains for privacy.

Once shut away in the little hut, I turned my back to Taylor so I wouldn't be tempted to look at her. I knew if I saw her naked breasts, it would all be over. I'd never have the strength to resist her.

"You can turn around now," she said with a sigh. My eyes drifted open and I realized I'd squeezed them shut as an extra layer of protection against ogling her. She was already on her belly, a simple cotton sheet covering her lower half. I removed my shirt and shorts and eased under my own sheet, glancing over at her once I was settled. Her arms were folded under her chin and the side of her breast was visible. I turned away quickly and focused on the table full of assorted oils and lotions. "This is so nice," she crooned, closing her eyes.

"They haven't even started yet," I chuckled.

"I know, but still," she offered. "It's nice out here. I just love the smell of the ocean and the sound of the waves. It's so tranquil."

It amazed me how simple it was to please her and make her happy. She didn't need extravagant gifts or shopping sprees or a reward for going scuba diving. She just enjoyed being there. She was a breath of fresh air.

"Thank you," she said, and my eyes drifted back to her. I was careful to keep them focused on her face and not let them dip any lower on her body. "I don't know if I've told you yet or not, but thanks for bringing me along. This place is beautiful." She glanced away. "I know I'm not the person you wanted to be here with," she began, and my chest tightened. I wanted to stop her and tell her she was wrong, but what she said was the truth. Taylor wasn't who I planned to bring here, but I was glad she was here with me. "But I'm still grateful you let me tag along. You planned an amazing vacation." Before she could say anything else, the curtains were pulled open and tied back. For the next sixty minutes, we received the most relaxing massage I'd ever had.

Dinner was being delivered and set up in our villa this evening, another event I planned ahead of time. We had just enough time to shower and get dressed before it showed up. A butler in a suit served us dinner, pouring us each a glass of wine before placing the bottle in ice to chill. I dismissed him, assuring him his services would not be needed until the meal was complete, and slipped him a generous tip.

"Wow, this is really impressive," Taylor announced, looking over the spread. Even though we stayed in for dinner, she still put on a little makeup and fixed her hair, styling her long tresses into soft waves and pinning one side back. She wore a dark blue maxi dress with giant hibiscus flowers printed on it. Her lips matched the dark pink flowers and I couldn't help but wonder how bad it would smear if I kissed her.

I tried to push those thoughts from my mind, needing to make it through dinner without getting worked up over her again. But she looked so amazing. Her tanned shoulders were now dusted in freckles, as were her nose and cheeks. Her hazel eyes shone in the soft candlelight our butler had insisted on providing, black lashes framing the gold flecked orbs. One side of her slender neck was exposed where her hair was swept back from her face. She was exquisite and I needed to stop staring.

"What is this?" Taylor asked as she dipped her spoon into her soup.

"That is lobster bisque."

"Mmm," she moaned when she placed it in her mouth and the sound went straight to my dick. *Shit, stay down. Stay down!* "This is delicious."

Oblivious to my inner turmoil, she continued to eat her soup, making little sounds of pleasure every so often. This was going to be one of the most uncomfortable dinners of my life if she didn't stop. Mercifully, she ate her orange roughy mostly in silence. We polished off the wine during dessert, leaving us with nothing to occupy our mouths. Mine longed to taste hers.

"What do you want to do now?" Taylor asked.

"I don't know. I didn't have anything planned for after dinner."

She gave me a coy smile and shook her head. "You don't have to plan *everything*. We can do something spontaneous, you know," she taunted.

"Like what?" I challenged, leaning forward and resting my elbows on the table, clasping my hands together.

She thought on that for a moment. "We could go back to that club," she offered, and I bristled. "Or just go out for drinks," she added quickly, noticing my reaction. "Somewhere a little more chill," she elaborated. "We're both dressed and ready for a night out. Might as well make the most of it." Her voice and expression were so hopeful, I couldn't have told her no if I wanted to. And I didn't.

We ended up in a high-end lounge that was a ten-minute walk from our villa. On the way over, I found myself reaching for her hand only to pull back before we could touch. It just felt so natural to want to hold her, to entwine my fingers with hers.

A waitress in black pants and a white top that buttoned all the way to her throat took our drink order, returning minutes later with two glasses, one filled with Stella and the other, a brightly colored concoction I didn't recognize. There was a group of people around our age lingering close by and we fell into easy conversation with them. They assumed Taylor and I were a couple, but I didn't correct them. It was easier to let them believe that than it was to explain the circumstances surrounding our joint vacation. Before the night was over, we made plans to join them for dinner and a show two nights from then.

I stopped at two beers, but continued to order Taylor whatever she wanted. She was getting tipsy and it was actually kind of cute. She got very giggly and very affectionate. She would lean into my side, wrapping her arms around my bicep and giving it a squeeze every time she laughed. I enjoyed it far more than I should have. When it was time to bid our new friends goodbye, she hugged them all, even the guys. One of them lingered far too long, his hand resting lower on her back than was appropriate. I ground my teeth together to keep from telling him to take his fucking hands off her.

We stopped to check out a few more places we hadn't yet visited before heading back to our villa. "I need to come back here earlier in the day so I can go shopping." Taylor stared longingly into the display window at a little boutique. "Oh my gosh, I neeeed those shoes!" she gushed, pressing her hand to the glass. I let out a soft laugh and hooked an arm around her, gently steering her away and back onto the street.

"You can come back and check it out tomorrow."

"Can I?" she asked, looking up at me with her big doe eyes.

In that moment, she looked so young and innocent, which made me feel even worse about all the salacious thoughts I'd been having about her. I released my steadying hold on her, pulling my hands away quickly like I'd been burned. She stumbled a bit and I prepared to catch her in case she fell, but she regained her balance easily. She was drunk, but not to the point of falling on her face and puking her guts out.

When we got back, I deposited Taylor in our bedroom and left quickly when she started to disrobe while I was still in the room. I shut the door behind me and went to the kitchen, grabbing a bottle of water and some pain relievers for her. She wasn't there when I returned, but the bathroom door was shut and I could hear water running, so I left them on her nightstand. I turned the TV on in the living room and made myself comfortable. I'd be sleeping on the couch again tonight. Taylor was already being more touchy-feely than normal because of the alcohol, and with her inhibitions lowered, I didn't want to take any chances and risk giving in to a temptation I wouldn't be able to fight.

ten

MY HEAD FELT A little fuzzy and there was a dull ache settling behind my eyes when I blinked them open. Sunlight poured in through the window and I pulled the blanket over my head to block it out. I wanted to just go back to sleep, but the bottle of water I chugged last night before passing out was pressing on my bladder insistently. Thank God Dalton had thought to bring it to me along with some medicine. I'd be in even worse shape if he hadn't. At the thought of Dalton, I removed the cover from my face and glanced at the spot next to me. Empty.

My heart sank. He didn't come to bed again last night. He was avoiding sleeping with me. Maybe that was for the best. Maybe we both needed a little space. I certainly needed to get my head on straight and stop fantasizing about him finally realizing he was madly in love with me and taking me to bed. I tiptoed into the main living area and saw Dalton curled up on the couch. He was most definitely too tall to be sleeping on it, but I wouldn't let myself feel bad for his discomfort. He had a perfectly good king-sized bed to sleep in if he so chose. It was his own damn fault if he wanted to be scrunched up on the couch.

I grabbed another bottle of water from the fridge and quietly prepared a slice of toast. My stomach felt okay, but I wasn't going to test the waters by putting anything too heavy on it after a night of drinking. After my simple breakfast, I brushed my teeth and washed my face before dressing in my favorite swimsuit. I'd purchased it just for this trip. It was a little skimpier than what I normally wore, but I'd always heard people were more relaxed and accepted the sight of a little more skin once you got outside the States.

I slipped into the Brazilian-cut bottoms and stood with my back to the full-length mirror, turning to look over my shoulder. It was a little out of my comfort zone to wear something like this, but I was pleased with how it looked. I typically worked out a few times a week and did hundreds of squats, so my butt was firm and round. The top was your average bikini top with thin straps, lined and slightly padded cups with underwire, and a back closure. I coated myself in sunscreen, grabbed my towel, and headed out to my lounger.

If Dalton wanted to join me when he woke up, he could, but I wasn't going to go out of my way to get him out here. An hour later, he appeared at my side, dressed in board shorts and holding a white paper bag from the cafe down the street.

"Hungry?" he asked.

"Depends," I responded playfully, and his lips quirked.

"On what?"

"Whatcha got in the bag?" I swung my legs around and sat up on the side of my chair. He opened it, the paper crinkling between his hands, and pulled out a beignet.

"Oooh, gimme!" I reached for it and he gave it up easily. "Mmm," I moaned, devouring the powdered sugar covered ball of fluffy fried dough. Beignets were my favorite. Did he know that somehow, or was this a happy coincidence?

"Chocolate milk?" he asked as he held out a small sealed plastic bottle.

"Thank you." It was like he read my mind.

We ate our sugar laden breakfast — my second breakfast — in silence. Once all the pastries and chocolate milk were gone, I offered to take all our trash inside and dispose of it. When I came back out, Dalton was spraying himself with sunscreen on the patio. I turned to shut the door behind me and heard him let out a low curse. Assuming he must have gotten some of the spray in his eyes, I turned quickly, ready to retrieve some water for him to flush it out. I wasn't prepared for what greeted me instead. Dalton's dark gaze seared into me, heating my skin. I shrank back into the corner of the patio as he stalked toward me.

"What the fuck are you wearing?" he growled, stopping only inches from me.

"What?"

"Don't play dumb with me. Ninety percent of your ass is on display for anyone to see."

His chest was heaving and so was mine, but his breath was coming hard and fast from anger, mine from arousal. Or maybe it was the other way around. He looked at me like he wanted to spank my ass and send me to bed for being defiant. *Or so he could ravage me.* The heated look in his eyes had my thighs clamping together, but his words made me spitting mad. *Who the fuck does he think he is?*

"It's a bathing suit," I seethed.

"It's a thong," he snapped.

"Wrong," I countered. "They're Brazilian cut," I corrected him.

His eyes flashed down my body and I knew what he was thinking. Was there anything else on my lower body that was *Brazilian?*

"You're practically naked," he growled, and the sound sent a pulse of arousal straight to my core. He leaned in closer, bracing his palm against the wall behind me. My heartbeat skyrocketed, the anticipation of a kiss stealing my already panting breath. "The only thing I *can't* see is your ass crack."

His crass statement should have smothered the flames of my lust, but all it did was fan them. I had to bite my tongue so I wouldn't ask if he wanted to see that, too.

His eyes moved to my mouth and I realized it wasn't my tongue I was biting, but my lip. He closed his eyes and leaned away from me, removing his hands from the wall. Taking a step back, he let out a pent-up breath and scrubbed his hands over his face.

"I thought after what happened the other day, you'd be more careful about how much of your," he stumbled for a second, swallowing thickly against what he wanted to say, "body you put on display."

I scowled and shoved past him. I wasn't going to let him shame me for wearing what I wanted. It didn't matter what his reasoning was, whether it was because of my brother or his misguided need to protect me. There was no way I was changing for him. If someone wanted to look at the perky little ass I worked hard for, let them. Look, but don't touch. That was my policy.

Except when it came to Dalton.

I flopped back down in my chair and shoved my sunglasses back down over my eyes. I was pouting. He made me feel small and self-conscious, and damn if that didn't turn me into even more of a brat. Maybe tomorrow, I *would* wear a thong. And go topless. See how he liked that.

He sidled up next to my chair and stared out at the ocean. I sat as still as a statue waiting to hear what he had to say. He took in a breath like he was preparing to speak, then let it out on a long sigh. Shaking his head, he walked into the ocean and dove under the water.

I adjusted my chair so it was flat and flopped over onto my stomach. It was time to turn over anyway, but it was also a satisfying way of giving him the middle finger by showing the barely covered ass cheeks he was just complaining about.

Dalton

I screwed up. Son of a bitch, I couldn't get anything right. Why did I have to open my big mouth and criticize Taylor's swimsuit?

I supposed because it was either that or rip it off her body and bend her over so I could see what lay hidden beneath that tiny scrap of fabric.

Why was I suddenly acting like a close-minded caveman? That wasn't me. I didn't tell women what they could and couldn't wear, so why was I treating Taylor like that? Maybe it was because I felt responsible for her. Aiden asked me to look after her and keep her safe, and I was afraid some dirtbag would get the wrong idea and try something with her if she was too exposed.

The more likely explanation was one I didn't want to admit. I wanted her for myself. I wanted to be the *only* one who got to see her like that. I wanted to be the only person with access to her most intimate parts. But she was off limits. Aiden made that perfectly clear.

When I saw that little bikini, I almost crossed that line and kissed her. With the tension between us multiplying every day, we would never make it through the rest of this trip without either killing each other or ending up in bed. I was screwed. We needed to put some distance between us. Maybe I could fly home early and let her enjoy the rest of this trip in peace.

Scratch that. I'd never leave her by herself in a foreign country. I'd already tried sleeping somewhere other than her bed, and all that accomplished was giving me a daily case of blue balls as a wake-up call. She invaded my dreams every night, so I couldn't even get a reprieve when I was asleep. Something had to give.

I was afraid we would explode like a firecracker shot into the air on the fourth of July, arcing until suddenly there were sparks and the night sky was momentarily on fire.

Eleven

Taylor

I WAS BEING SNEAKY.

Dalton was in the shower, so it was the perfect time to slip out of the villa undetected to do my own thing. After our heated conversation about my choice of swimwear, I stayed out on the beach most of the day, alternating between sunbathing and prancing around in the sand and water. It may have been a teeny, tiny bit intentional just to get under Dalton's skin, but I was still a bit salty about the whole thing. I finally came inside in the late afternoon, took a shower, and got ready. I spent a little extra time on my makeup and slipped on my favorite sundress. It was time to go exploring without my warden, and I wanted to look nice in case I encountered a man less concerned with policing my wardrobe and more concerned with getting underneath it.

I slid my feet into my sandals and grabbed my wristlet, slipping quietly out the door. My first stop was to the little shop with the shoes I was gushing over last night. I went inside, found my size, and bought them along with some locally made, handcrafted jewelry. When my stomach started to growl, I stopped at a little shack-like restaurant and ordered shrimp tacos. My phone buzzed with a new message and I glanced at the screen.

Dalton: Where are you?

Me: Out.

I kept my response vague. I didn't want him to come looking for me. This was my chance to get away from him and the constant electric attraction that drew me to him like a moth to a flame.

Dalton: I gathered that. Tell me where you are and I'll come to you.

Me: I'm just out exploring. I'll be back later.

Still keeping it vague.

Three little dots flashed across my phone for several seconds before disappearing, but no message showed up. I had my finger on the button to shut down my screen when the dots returned, and I stilled my hand. They quickly disappeared again. He'd been trying to think of the right thing to say but couldn't. Perhaps I had him shook. *Good.*

I meandered through the streets, stopping at almost all the shops and purchasing a few more items. Checking the time, I noticed a missed call from Dalton and a text time-stamped a few minutes later.

Dalton: Want to grab dinner?

Me: Thanks, but I already ate.

Several minutes went by before his response came through.

Dalton: If you change your mind, I'm at Shells & Shakes.

I smiled at his choice of cuisine. It was the same place I'd eaten at earlier.

Me: Get the shrimp tacos. They're delicious.

Dalton: Will do. Thanks for the tip.

He punctuated the message with a smiling emoji and I instantly relaxed. It felt like things were returning to normal. We weren't arguing or fighting the sexual tension that had been mounting between us. I guess we both just needed some space.

The sun was dipping low in the sky and the nightly entertainers were preparing for shows. I watched as colorfully dressed dancers moved to authentic island music. Women garbed in fuchsia, orange, and saffron feathered headdresses shimmied and swayed to a catchy drumbeat and I clapped in time with the rhythm. I watched for a while, enjoying the sights and sounds and colorful clothing before deciding to take a walk on the beach. There were several bars and restaurants butted up to the beach, so I took my shoes off and sank my toes into the sand. It was cool to the touch and powdery soft.

I was nearing the villa when a quaint, straw hut bar caught my eye. The entire oceanfront side was open, so I stepped inside and glanced around. Only half the bar was occupied, but all the patrons seemed to be having a good time. Some sipped colorful drinks while others held glasses of wine or mugs of beer. It seemed like the perfect place to stop and have a drink.

"Taylor?" a familiar deep voice called.

I followed the sound to the bar and found Nico standing behind it, rinsing a glass. *He worked here?* I thought he was a tourist like me when I met him at the club. He seemed like a wealthy businessman, so polite, confident, and incredibly well dressed, a very desirable combination.

I walked up and took a seat on one of the bar stools, a growing smile spreading over my lips. "Hey!" I greeted him. "I didn't know you worked here."

He smiled and ducked his head. "Yeah," he said a little shyly. "Gotta pay for college somehow," he offered, his bright, beaming smile never faltering.

"Nothing wrong with that," I praised, gaining a new respect for him. Anybody who had to work their way through college and didn't have someone else to foot the bill deserved some credit.

"What are you drinking tonight, pretty lady?"

I blushed, enjoying his attention and compliment. "What's your specialty?" I asked, an air of flirtation in my voice. Maybe Nico was just what I needed to get Dalton out of my system. I'd never been one for random hookups or one night stands, but spending a night or two in Nico's bed and never seeing him again would be less shameful and embarrassing than the entirety of my most recent relationship.

My smile fell as I thought about Jason and his deception. No. I wouldn't think of him tonight. I'd managed to push him *and* the fallout of our disastrous love affair from my mind all week. I refused to let that poison seep in and taint my evening.

Nico held up a finger in a "give me a second" gesture and turned to face the shelf full of liquor bottles behind the bar. He pulled a couple bottles out, pouring a little of each into a glass before adding a scoop of ice and some blue cocktail mix. He gave it a stir, popped an orange on the rim, and slid it across the bar. I took a tentative sip. It was sweet and a little tangy with a hint of citrus.

"This is really good," I praised.

"Thank you. I call it 'Nico Juice'."

My face warmed at the suggestive name and I knew my cheeks were probably bright pink. I took a large gulp of the cold drink to cool me down and hide my blush.

I sat at the bar for a long time, talking to Nico about everything from school to jobs and hobbies. He continued to serve other customers but always came back to me, and we'd pick up where we left off.

We were laughing about a story Nico was telling me about a patron he'd recently found passed out behind the bar when he glanced up and the smile fell from his face.

"Your friend's here." He nodded past me and I turned in my seat. Dalton was watching us, his jaw set tight like he'd caught me doing something wrong. He walked up to the bar and got in front of me, doing his best to block my view of my new friend.

"I've been looking everywhere for you." His voice was calm and steady, belying the tension I felt rolling off him in waves.

"I didn't realize I was required to check in with you," I replied sweetly, sipping my drink. His eyes dropped to the glass and his brow furrowed.

"What the hell is that?"

"It's Nico Juice." I knew what calling Nico's signature drink by its name would do to Dalton's already fiery temper, but I couldn't help myself. I was having a good time, and would potentially have had an even better time with my new acquaintance later tonight before Dalton walked in and clam-jammed me.

The muscles in his jaw flexed but he kept his composure. He calmly took the drink from me, set it on the bar, threw down a hundred-dollar bill, and grabbed my hand. The unexpected contact sent a shockwave up my arm, and it took me until we were several yards down the beach to come to my senses and yank my hand free of his.

"What is wrong with you?" I seethed. "I was having a good time."

"You don't even know that guy. He could've slipped something into your drink."

"You're being ridiculous." I rolled my eyes and tried to move past him back to the bar. "He made those drinks right in front of me."

His arm shot out and he caught me around the waist. "He's a stranger. You need to stay away from him."

"Stop telling me what to do!" I shouted and tried to rush past him again, but I didn't get far. He grabbed me and in one fluid motion, he crouched down and hoisted me into the air. I let out a "humph" when my stomach landed on his shoulder.

"Put me down, you Neanderthal!" I demanded, kicking my legs.

"If you're going to act like a child, then I'm going to treat you like one," he bellowed, and I gasped. "Brat," he mumbled under his breath.

I was frozen in stunned disbelief. Was this real life? Was Dalton James seriously carrying me over his shoulder like I was a petulant, uncontrollable child?

I shivered when I realized his hand was braced high up on the back of my thigh. If he slid it just a couple inches higher, his fingers could be in my panties. He nodded to someone and greeted them with a quick hello, jolting me from my fantasy. What the hell was wrong with me that I could think about *that* in a time like *this*? The couple stopped and turned to look at me when

Dalton passed them by. I gave them a little wave so they wouldn't be tempted to intervene or call security.

When they were out of earshot, I growled, "Put me down." Dalton ignored me and kept walking.

"I said, *put me down*," I commanded louder this time, wiggling out of his grasp.

"Hold still," he ordered and gripped my leg tighter. The sensation was too much, a mix of arousal and frustration.

"Dalton James, you put me down this instant, or so help me-" I didn't get to finish my threat because I was unceremoniously dropped onto the sand, landing ungracefully on my ass.

I stood and brushed the sand from my skirt before lunging at him. "You son of a bitch!" I shouted, shoving at his chest, but he gripped my shoulders and held me at arm's length "What is your problem?"

"Calm down, Taylor."

"Calm down? You just ruined my night! I had plans."

His eyes narrowed into slits and a murderous expression slid over his face. "What were you planning to do?"

I threw his arm off and stepped back. "What do you care?" He winced and shoved his fingers into his hair. All that did was make it even more perfectly disheveled, adding to his already off-the-charts sex appeal.

"I promised your brother-"

"No," I cut him off. "Don't make this about Aiden," I warned. "We are both adults and are free to make our own choices. I wouldn't stop you from doing something you wanted to do. I deserve the same consideration." He gripped the back of his neck in frustration, conflicting emotions warring over his features. "Or do you think since you paid for all this," I began, motioning around us with my hands, "that you have some say over what I do while we're here?"

His eyes widened and snapped to my face. "God, no. I would never think that."

"Then what is it? Because if you met someone you liked and wanted to go back to their room and have a little fun, I wouldn't try to stop you." Even though the mere thought sent pain spearing through my chest. It would destroy me, but I wouldn't have any say in it. Any man in his position would be ready for some no-strings-attached hooking up in a tropical paradise after practically being left at the altar. I wouldn't blame him, even though I'd be heartbroken.

"Hell, you could've hooked up with that flight attendant who was giving you googly eyes the whole plane ride while I was asleep, and there's nothing I could say about it, because *it's none of my business*." I said the last five words slowly, hoping my meaning would sink in, even though the thought of him screwing her in the first-class bathroom made me want to throw up.

"She offered," he said in a quiet voice.

"What?" I asked, stunned. I really didn't want to know any more, didn't want to hear about what he did with her, but the question was out of my mouth before I could reel it back in.

"That flight attendant," he began, and I fought the urge to slap my hands over his mouth, "propositioned me. Offered to blow me," he elaborated. Bile churned in my stomach. Here I'd been fantasizing about him the last four days, and he'd gotten some on the plane ride over. "But I turned her down."

My eyes snapped to his and I noticed they were so bright and intense, even in the moonlight. "Why?" *Shut up, Taylor. Stop asking these questions. You might not like the answers.*

"Because I didn't want her." He moved closer to me, so close I had to tilt my chin back to maintain eye contact. "I wanted *you*."

I opened my mouth to speak, but no sound came out because his lips were on mine. One hand cupped my face, his fingertips spearing into my hair as his other arm wrapped around my waist, crushing me to him. My lips parted on a moan and his tongue slipped inside. *This* was the moment I'd waited for since that fateful night in his SUV all those years ago.

It was over all too soon and I fought back a whimper. He brushed the hair away from my face and studied me. "I've always wanted you," he confessed, and my knees almost gave out.

"Wh-what?" I asked, dumbfounded.

"I've wanted to do that for so long," he admitted, closing his eyes and pressing his forehead to mine. "Ever since that night I drove you home from the ball game," he began, but shook his head. "No, even before that," he clarified. "But your brother made me promise I wouldn't go after you. He warned me to stay away and I respected him, respected his wishes," he said, pain flashing in his eyes. "But I can't keep that promise anymore." He looked into my eyes, begging me for confirmation that I wanted this, too.

For the first time since I was fifteen years old, riding shotgun in his car, I closed the short distance between our mouths and kissed him. He groaned into it and squeezed me harder. His hand tangled in my hair and the tension I'd been feeling since we got on that plane four days ago melted away.

His lips crashed over mine, matching the rhythm of the waves pounding against the shore. He nipped and tasted, drawing my body as close to him as possible. The hard ridge of his arousal pressed against my belly and I moaned into his mouth. He groaned and lifted me into his arms. My legs clamped around his torso as his hands gripped my ass and he began to walk.

Somehow, we made it back to our villa without ever breaking our kiss. We ignored the front door and walked right up to our back patio. He carried me inside and slid the door closed behind us. My back hit the mattress and he settled his hips between mine. The press of his erection against my already wet center had my back arching off the bed.

Dalton kissed his way from my mouth to my chest, brushing his lips gently over my chin and jaw, his tongue darting out to taste the skin covering my throat. The front of my dress was yanked down, exposing my bra as the thin straps fell down my arms.

"Fuck," he groaned when he pushed the cups down, exposing my breasts. His head dipped and he took one pink tip in his mouth, sucking gently.

"Ah!" I cried out in pleasure. He swirled his tongue around the stiffening peak and my hands came up to grip his hair. He lavished that breast before moving to the next and paying it equal attention. He finally slid down my body and lifted my dress, fingering the edge of my panties.

"I've been dreaming about what you would taste like every night," he confessed, hooking his finger inside the elastic and tracing it all the way down the front panel. My muscles clenched as the back of his finger brushed against me, dampening his skin with my arousal. "I wake up so hard thinking about this sweet," he began, pushing my panties aside and pushing one finger into my body, "tight pussy."

I gasped at the sensation and his naughty words. His finger worked in and out of me a few times before sliding up to circle around my clit. My eyes closed, my head pressing back into the mattress as he continued the euphoric motion.

"If you want me to stop, tell me now before this goes any further," Dalton warned, sliding his finger back inside me. Once my walls were generously lubricated, he slipped a second finger inside and curled them forward.

"No!" I cried, a little too loud. A smile curved his lips, his expression pleased. "Don't stop," I pleaded breathlessly. He removed his fingers and I almost shouted at him to put them back, but the words caught in my throat when he started sliding my panties down my legs. *Never mind. Carry on, sir.*

He watched my face as he slid the fabric past one foot and then the other. Leaning down, he sealed his mouth over mine, kissing me with a ferocity I'd never experienced before. When he leaned back up, his eyes traveled down my body and his pleased expression warmed my skin. I lay there with my dress pulled down and breasts exposed, the skirt hiked up around my waist, and my bottom half completely bare. He looked at me like I was the most beautiful woman he'd ever seen, like a starving man admiring a feast before taking his first taste.

His head finally descended, and his lips pressed against my hip bone. I tried to be patient, but my hips began to twist of their own accord, angling my center to his skillful mouth. He chuckled against my skin, my impatience having no effect on his pace. He took his time teasing me, tempting me, increasing my need with every passing second before finally, gloriously, his tongue flicked against my tender bud. I arched off the bed, nearly coming at the first lick after what felt like hours of waiting. His fingers returned to my opening and pressed inside. My orgasm crashed over me quickly, my body trembling with aftershocks.

He kissed his way back up to my breast and stayed there a moment before returning to my lips. "Sit up," he instructed gently, and I complied. He unhooked my bra and tossed it aside before tugging my dress up and over my head. Once it was removed, my hair fell in soft waves around my shoulders, concealing my breasts. He pushed the tresses back over my shoulders, exposing me to him once again.

"You're even more perfect than I imagined," he praised, admiring my naked form.

Was I dreaming? Did Dalton just call me perfect? This was every teenage fantasy I'd ever had coming true. While most girls were drooling over Taylor Lautner and Channing Tatum, I was dreaming of offering my V-card to Dalton and hoping he'd be the only man to know me intimately.

I finally realized he was still fully clothed. That needed to be remedied immediately. I reached for the hem of his shirt and pushed the material up, exposing his taut abs. My tongue darted out to wet my lips and I yearned to lick over every bump of his six—no, make that eight—pack. He grabbed the collar of his shirt and pulled it the rest of the way off. I reached for his fly as his hands landed on the button, and together, we had his shorts undone in seconds. I slid them the rest of the way off and he kicked them aside.

Impatiently, I pushed his briefs down over his hips, exposing his impressive erection. I gulped at the size of it, my mouth watering at the same time, eager to taste. I wrapped my hand around the shaft and looked up at him. He watched me with rapt attention, tenderly brushing the hair from my face. I couldn't wait to make him feel as good as he made me feel.

I opened my mouth, covering my bottom teeth and lip with my tongue, and took him in. He hissed out a breath and his fingers tightened in my hair. Holy shit, this was hot.

"Taylor. Fuck." His voice was strained, but in the best way possible. I worked him over, stroking him with my hand, gliding my lips and tongue up and down his shaft.

"Taylor," he breathed my name. "Taylor, you're going to have to stop."

Why on earth would he want me to stop? I thought he was enjoying this.

He tugged on my hair gently and I let him pop free. He lifted me with one arm around my back and the other hooked behind my knee and placed me in the middle of the bed. His body covered mine, his cock brushing against my core.

Oh, shit.

He ground his hips, sliding his erection against my slick flesh. "I need to be inside you," he growled, and I suddenly understood why he made me stop.

He pulled away and jumped off the bed, grabbing his pants off the floor and pulling his wallet from a pocket. He retrieved a square foil packet and returned to the bed, tearing it open with his teeth. I watched, enthralled as he placed the rubber sheath on his tip and rolled it down his length. That was going to be in me.

Oh my God, this was really happening. I was finally getting what I'd wanted all these years, and it was even more glorious than I could have imagined.

With protection in place, he settled between my legs and wasted no time devouring my mouth with a sultry kiss, his tongue diving in and tangling with mine. I felt him at my entrance and lifted my hips, urging him forward, encouraging him to finally take the plunge. And he did. Oh, glorious delayed gratification! This was the sex I'd been trying to have for the past eight years.

He eased into me, giving my body a chance to adjust to his size. "You're so fucking tight," he said, his voice gruff and thick with need and restraint. It felt like he was about to split me in half, but it was the most pleasurable pain I'd ever felt. He started moving, his hips pulsing in and out. Every few strokes, he eased in a little further and each time I wondered, *How can there be more?* But there always was.

He looked down at me wearing an expression I'd never seen on him before. His eyes scrolled over me, taking in every detail of my face. I watched until my eyes fluttered closed and my next orgasm started to build. He picked up his pace, bringing me closer to release with every stroke, and when I came apart, he wasn't far behind.

twelve

AIDEN WAS GOING TO kill me.

I fucked his little sister. Ugh, why did that have to sound so taboo? She was an adult, a grown woman capable of making her own decisions and having sex with whomever she chose. She just happened to choose me, the one person forbidden to touch her. This was *not* going to go over well. He was bound to find out because, quite frankly, I planned on doing it again. And again. And again. In fact, I hoped to make it a regular occurrence.

My mind raced as I laid there holding Taylor while she slept. We were both naked and I could feel her smooth, bare skin against mine. She felt good curled into my side, my arm cradled around her shoulders, her head resting in the crook of mine. I'd waited *years* for this. I just hoped I hadn't jeopardized my friendship with Aiden.

I mean, he set those boundaries when we were teenagers. Surely he didn't still expect me to honor them. Taylor didn't need his protection anymore. He was no longer warding off the horndogs we went to high school with. Taylor was smart and capable of choosing a partner based on her own wants and needs. I just hoped he would be able to see that and didn't cut my dick off when I got home, after he inevitably found out I hooked up with her.

I closed my eyes and tried to calm my racing mind. We had another adventure-filled day ahead of us and I needed to get some rest. Hopefully our day would start with more horizontal aerobics.

I got my wish when I woke up the next morning. Taylor's small, soft hand pressed to the center of my chest and my pulse accelerated under her touch. She slowly slid it down my abdomen, the muscles tightening as she brushed over them. Her touch was electric. My skin tingled everywhere she touched me, a current of desire passing through her hand and landing between my legs. I rose to the occasion quickly, and when she reached for me, I was hard and ready. She moaned into my throat when her fingers wrapped around my cock. I fought the urge to thrust my hips into her grasp, digging my fingers into her hip.

I breathed her in, basking in the sweet scent of vanilla and coconut that permeated the air. There was something else that clung to her skin, barely detectable past her own delicious aroma. There were notes of spice and bergamot, a mixture I was all too familiar with. It was *my* scent clinging to her body, holding on as proof that we'd shared an intimate connection. And I fucking loved it.

The moment I'd fantasized about for years finally became reality. I'd forgotten just how badly I wanted her. I'd loved Gianna and was loyal to only her when we were together. Any time thoughts of Taylor started to creep in, I would push them from my mind and focus on the woman with whom I planned to spend the rest of my life. Now that I had Taylor, I realized those fantasies didn't have shit on the real thing.

I pulled her on top of me and she straddled my hips. Her grip remained on my solid length and she continued to pump. Her lips were pink and pouty from my kiss and her skin was flushed.

"I need to be inside you," I confessed, and her eyes fluttered closed.

"I need that, too." Her voice was soft and wispy, barely audible past the blood rushing in my ears.

"Hold on," I instructed and slid from beneath her. I located my suitcase in the walk-in closet, digging for the small cardboard box I'd packed just in case. I hadn't planned on using them with Taylor, but I hadn't planned *not* to, either.

When I got on that plane five days ago, I had no expectations concerning my travelling companion. I was still licking my wounds, my heart and ego battered and bruised by Gianna's betrayal. It still stung when I thought of her, but it no longer made the center of my chest ache. Taylor was healing me. She was everything I wanted but didn't know I needed.

I finally pulled the condoms free and headed back to the bed. Thankfully, I'd had one in my wallet last night and didn't have to do a search and recover mission just to find one. It was a good thing, because I might have done something stupid in the heat of the moment. That thought sobered me, reminding me to make an appointment with my doctor to get checked when I got home. Gianna had been cheating on me, and although she never came right out and admitted to sleeping with him, I knew she had. I wasn't stupid. A woman didn't call off her wedding the week of her nuptials for a man she hadn't taken for a test drive yet.

That thought gave me pause. Was he better than me? She always seemed quite satisfied with our sex life, so I never considered she might be looking elsewhere for what I wasn't giving her. *That* was a blow to my ego, and now I was letting my cheating ex fiancé ruin my morning with the fantastic woman I shared a bed with last night.

I looked up and all thoughts of Gianna evaporated. Taylor was sitting up on the bed on her knees, her hair mussed and cascading around her shoulders. Her eyes drank me in and she licked her lips. I did the same. She was completely naked, her beautiful body on full display. She was perfect. Her breasts were full and perky and tipped with the prettiest shade of pink. Her skin was bronzed and just a tiny bit freckled. Her bright hazel eyes seemed to glow as she watched me stalk back to the bed. They were full of desire and something a little deeper, something that resembled long-held adoration.

Something akin to affection tightened around my heart, lacing itself through every chamber. I'd known this woman most of my life, grew up with her, had her throw herself at me as a teenager, only to be forced to reject her. Not anymore. I couldn't resist her any longer, my friendship with Aiden be damned.

I reached for her, sliding my hand to the back of her head and tangling my fingers into the hair at her nape. My lips caught hers and I poured the last eight years of longing into our kiss. Her hands came up to my shoulders as I wrapped my free arm around her waist and crushed her to me. My body ignited, my skin aflame everywhere she touched me.

We sank down onto the mattress, a tangle of limbs and tongues. She pushed against my chest, straddling my hips as my back hit the sheets. She knew exactly what she wanted and there was no stopping her from getting it. But why the hell would I want to?

When I ripped the foil open, she took it from me and eagerly slid the rubber down my shaft. My head fell back and I groaned at the sensation of her hands on me. I opened them just as she angled her body over mine, lining my full arousal up with her entrance. Our eyes locked as she lowered herself down onto my length. Her lips parted with a gasp and I fought to keep my eyes open so I could watch her. She moved her hips, rocking back and forth, a soft moan escaping as she braced herself on my abdomen. My hands splayed over the tops of her thighs, gripping her tightly. Her breasts bounced, the motion completely mesmerizing. I let my hands drift up her sides and settle on her breasts, gently kneading and caressing them. Her hands came up and settled on the backs of mine and she squeezed, encouraging me to keep touching her. I brushed my thumbs over her nipples, watching them pebble before rolling and tugging them. She moaned and arched into my touch.

I pumped into her, taking over and setting a new rhythm. She started groaning and making the same sexy noises she made last night just before she came. I released one breast and found her clit with my thumb, circling it, slow at first and then faster, matching the speed of my thrusts. She fell apart, crying out with her release. I stilled soon after, finding my own climax, and her head fell to my chest. It took us several minutes to catch our breath and collect ourselves. I cupped her face, bringing her lips to mine. It was a slow, sweet kiss and I savored it. I wanted to remember this moment, this point in time where no one else existed but us. Where we were hundreds of miles from home, secluded in our own little paradise.

"What do you have in store for us today?" Taylor asked as we sat at the island eating fresh fruit and scrambled eggs.

"We have the dolphin encounter," I began, glancing at my watch, "in less than an hour. Then there's this waterfall near there I'd like to check out." I sent her a sly grin and her face flushed. I had a feeling she knew exactly what I wanted to check out beneath that waterfall. "This evening, we're booked for a sunset cruise, then dinner and a show with the group we met the other night."

So much had changed since that night. I was no longer fighting my attraction for her. I wasn't avoiding her body as though her touch would sear my skin. I'd been set ablaze by her, deep inside where the flames of my desire raged, but I no longer shied away from her touch. I craved it, greedily seeking it out at every opportunity. Even now, while we ate, I had my hand on her knee, my thumb rubbing over the bony protrusion.

"Wow, we're going to have a busy day. That all sounds amazing."

Once our breakfast was finished and the dishes were washed up, we got ready and headed to our first destination of the day. I watched as Taylor removed her little cotton shorts and tank top, revealing her swimsuit. She'd chosen something with a bit more coverage this time and I was both thankful *and* disappointed.

Her face lit up when a dolphin swam right up to her as soon as we were submerged in the water. She reached out a hand and gently stroked its snout and the top of its head. She giggled as it bobbed its head up and down and splashed her in the face. In that moment, I was eternally grateful that it was her here with me and nobody else. Gianna would have hated this. She would've fussed and made a scene because her makeup would be ruined. Taylor, on the other hand, was fresh faced and completely bare, save for some lip balm and sunscreen. She looked adorable with her long hair piled on top of her head in a messy bun, her light smattering of freckles on full display.

I had to stop making these comparisons. I needed to let go of Gianna and stop letting memories of her leach into the here and now. She was my past. Taylor was… well, she was my present. I couldn't think about what the future would hold. It had been irrevocably altered in the last week. All I could think about was right now, where Taylor was front and center.

We waded in the water, playing with the dolphins until our time was up. Taylor stuck her bottom lip out in a pout when we had to get out and dry off. I chuckled and pulled her into my arms, kissing her head. She was so cute and so much damn fun to be around. I never wanted this trip to end.

The waterfall wasn't far from where we'd played with the dolphins. I was surprised to find the area nearly empty, but also thrilled at the prospect of having a little privacy. Despite our efforts to dry off after swimming with the dolphins, our swimsuits remained damp. The hem of my light blue shirt darkened with the water seeping into it from my board shorts. The flimsy cotton material covering Taylor's body clung to her just like *I* wanted to, hugging the curves and valleys, dipping between her breasts and legs. Good Lord, I was jealous of her clothes. I swallowed hard, suppressing a groan when she peeled the damp cotton from her hips and down her legs. I had to turn away and think of something else before I embarrassed myself.

The water was cooler here than in the ocean. There was more shade and a constant flow, but it was refreshing against the humid tropical climate. We jumped right in, Taylor squealing at the unexpected coldness. We splashed around, drawing closer to the falls, and Taylor gasped as chilly drops of water peppered her bare skin. I grabbed a hold of her and pulled her against my chest.

"I'll keep you warm," I promised against her lips. My actions ignited a firestorm of lust. The gold flecks of her irises glowed like a flame before she closed her eyes and pressed her lips to mine. Our tongues met and a slow dance of seduction ensued. Her arms wrapped around my neck and she drew me in closer, pressing her breasts against my chest. My arms tightened around her middle, my hands splaying over her back. We kissed until we were both breathless and I was hard. The water was mercifully up to our chests now, hiding the proof of my arousal pressed against her belly.

"Dalton," she breathed when the connection was broken. Our chests heaved like we'd just finished running a marathon.

"Let's get out of here." It was supposed to be a suggestion, but it came out low and gruff like a command. This was fun, and I hated to miss out on enjoying more of this beautiful landscape, but I needed her. It didn't matter that I'd had her only hours earlier. She kept me on edge, ready to lay her down and bury myself to the hilt at the drop of a hat.

Thirteen

AFTER WE MADE LOVE for the second time today, we spent a lazy afternoon lounging on the beach. We had lunch delivered and enjoyed it on the patio, watching as the waves rolled in and crashed against the shore. Our cruise didn't start for a few more hours, so we had plenty of time to relax and soak up the sun before getting ready for the evening. We dozed off, the sound of the ocean lulling us into an afternoon nap. Our bodies were overly warm when we awoke so we took a dip in the clear blue water to cool off, wading lazily out to sea, hand in hand.

Dalton slid his arms around me, settling one hand low on my back, just above my ass while the other settled between my shoulder blades, pressing our chests closer together. He felt like a dream, our bodies connected from thighs to chest. His lips met mine in a gentle, languorous kiss. He took his time, tasting and exploring every corner of my mouth.

We stayed on the beach until it was time to get ready for the evening. When we finally came inside, I hopped in the shower first so I'd have time to get ready. I was rinsing conditioner from my hair when a cool gust of air hit my wet skin. I swiped a hand over my face, removing the excess water from my eyes before opening them. Dalton stood in front of me, his hooded eyes scanning down my body. He stepped inside the shower and I finally noticed he was naked. And oh, so hard. I gulped, the sight of him in all his glorious, naked perfection making it suddenly hard to breathe or swallow.

He closed the glass door behind him and wordlessly stepped up to me, his tall frame towering above me. His arms encased my torso and his mouth descended on mine, his tongue gliding over the seam of my lips. I willingly granted him access. When he rolled his hips and his erection slid against my damp skin, I groaned into his kiss as the water cascaded over our bodies.

He pulled back, a glint of mischief shining in his deep brown eyes. His hands slid around to my front, one gripping my hip while the other trailed slowly up my side to cup my breast. My breath left me in a whoosh when his thumb brushed over the tender bud. It puckered as he circled it, coaxing it into a stiff peak.

His head descended, his hot mouth replacing his hand, and my eyes closed as my arms came up to frame his shoulders. One hand slid into his hair, gripping it tightly, and I felt him smile against my skin. His hand skimmed down my belly, his fingers following the thin trail of curls before sinking into the inviting warmth that awaited him. My head fell back and a moan escaped my lips. He pressed me backwards until my shoulder blades connected with the cold tile and I gasped. His mouth left my breast and he knelt in front of me. He watched himself pleasure me for a moment and my inner muscles clamped around his finger. The act was so erotic, and I felt vulnerable with him staring at the most intimate part of my body, but it was so incredibly sexy.

My skin heated, my belly tightening in anticipation. When he finally leaned in and took a long, slow lick, I cried out. The sensation was overwhelming, but I wanted him to do it again. I got my wish. He came back, returning to my clit and ravishing it with his hot tongue while his fingers curled forward inside me. My legs began to shake, and I feared I would collapse. He lifted one weak-kneed leg and threw it over his shoulder, his hand sliding up the back of my thigh to cradle my ass for support. It didn't take long for my orgasm to explode and my cries of pleasure to echo around us.

Dalton let my leg fall back to the ground and held onto me as I steadied myself. His mouth found my shoulder and he trailed kisses all the way to my lips. His body pressed into mine as I wrapped my arms around his neck, pulling him into me. I couldn't wait to return the favor. I let my hands relax and slide back over his shoulders, giving them a gentle shove, breaking our kiss. He gave me a perplexed look, unsure why I would push him away, but I just let my hands continue to drift further down his body, across his chest and over the hard ridges of his stomach. His gaze lowered and he watched as I explored his body.

His erection bobbed and flexed when my hands were only inches away. I loved how he anticipated my touch. I gripped him in my hand and he groaned, bracing a hand against the wall behind me. I stroked him a few times before dropping to my knees. He sucked in a breath as my body lowered to the tile floor.

"Taylor." My name came out on a pant, the sound of a man desperate for my touch. I opened my mouth and eased my lips over the crown. He groaned, the needy sound spurring me on. He was big, and there was no way I could take him all in, but I would take him as deep as I could. I kept my hand wrapped around the base, stroking in rhythm with my sucks. A low rumbling sound vibrated in his chest as I worked him over, not a grunt, but not quite a growl. It was primal and sexy, and I wanted to keep hearing it. His hips began making short little thrusts as his hand settled into my hair.

"Taylor, fuck. I'm gonna–" The warning fell from his lips as hot bursts of liquid hit the back of my throat. I finished him off and was instantly lifted to my feet and wrapped in a tight embrace. His chest was heaving as he tried to catch his breath. "Sorry about that," he spoke into my hair, smoothing his palm over it. "That one just kind of snuck up on me."

"It's fine," I chuckled. I normally wasn't a fan of that, but with Dalton, it didn't bother me in the least. He let out a relieved laugh and framed my face with his hands, kissing me softly on the lips.

"I'd better let you out of here so you can get ready. I won't be long," he assured me.

With one final kiss, I slipped out of the shower and dried off, wrapping the towel around me and securing it just above my breasts. I combed through my hair and applied a little product to give it beachy waves before starting on my makeup. I'd been keeping it pretty light lately, but decided to go for a more dramatic, romantic look, considering the evening ahead. A sunset cruise with Dalton by my side sounded like a dream and I wanted to look perfect for it.

When Dalton stepped out, rubbing a towel over his chiseled torso, I gawked. I couldn't help myself. He was just so perfect. His body was incredibly well maintained and his muscles well defined. I considered myself one lucky girl to have the privilege of seeing him naked.

"See something you like?" he said to my reflection, a cocky grin revealing gleaming white teeth.

I see something I love.

Whoa, Nelly! I'd better put the brakes on that thought. Things had moved at lightning speed since he confessed he'd wanted me for years, but that was taking it too far, too fast. I buried those thoughts as deeply as I could and smiled into the mirror.

"I think you already know the answer to that," I responded playfully.

He regrettably wrapped the towel around his waist, hiding that glorious piece of manhood, and stalked up behind me. He leaned down and pressed a sweet kiss to my shoulder and I momentarily let my eyes close, basking in his affection. This man would be my undoing. I was treading dangerous waters here, but I wouldn't take a life raft now if someone threw me one.

"I'll let you finish getting ready. Wouldn't want to cause any distractions," he smirked and swatted my behind before exiting the bathroom.

Good Lord, what have I gotten myself into?

The sunset cruise was everything I imagined it would be and more. They served us drinks and hors d'oeuvres as we snuggled up together on a padded bench seat. I'd chosen an off-the-shoulder maxi dress with a slit up one side that exposed one leg when I crossed them. We sat at an angle in our seat, my back leaned up against his shoulder and his arm wrapped around my waist. Every few minutes, he pressed a kiss to my bare shoulder and

I'd close my eyes, overcome with euphoria at the sensation. I couldn't imagine how awkward this night would have been if we were still fighting our attraction to one another. We'd have to sit on opposite ends of the boat just to avoid touching and combusting into sexually repressed flames. Thank goodness that wasn't the case.

I rested my head against his large bicep and his arm curled even tighter around my waist. He pressed a kiss to my hair and nuzzled his face into my neck. My desire sparked to life with his affectionate touch, and he must have sensed the shift. The hand resting against my belly dropped to my leg and found the opening in my dress. His fingers brushed over the sensitive skin covering my thigh and I held my breath, wondering what he would do next.

I glanced around, hoping nobody would notice what he was doing. Thankfully, there weren't many others on this boat and the people who were there were with their partners and paying us no mind.

Dalton's fingers pushed the gauzy material higher, finding the edge of my panties. He dipped beneath them, tracing the seam from the crease of my leg up to my hip and back down.

"I can't wait to tear these off of you," he growled into my ear. "Now that I know just how sweet you taste, I may have to use my teeth."

My breath hitched and my thighs clamped together as heat and desire flooded between my legs. How far would he go? How intimately would he touch me with other people around? I almost uncrossed my legs just to tempt him and find out, but he lowered his hand, splaying his palm over my thigh and squeezing.

"Later," he promised on a whisper.

When the cruise was over, we walked along the well-lit beach, mingling with other guests. This area of the resort was where the party was. Couches, loungers, and even beds were grouped around fire pits with tiki torches illuminating the spaces between. People were laughing and drinking, all dressed in clothes a little too fancy for the beach.

"Want to grab a drink?" Dalton asked, nodding toward the bar overlooking the water from a manmade stone pier. It was shaped like an octagon with a three hundred sixty-degree view of the ocean and the bar situated in the very center.

"That sounds great." We walked along the short pier with our hands laced together. We each ordered a drink and found seats at the crowded counter. "What time is dinner?"

Dalton consulted his watch before answering. "We've got about twenty minutes. We can head that way when we finish our drinks," he offered, holding up his half empty glass.

We bumped into the group we were having dinner with as we left the beach and followed them the few blocks to the restaurant where they'd made reservations. The hostess didn't seem to mind the additions to their party and led us to the hibachi grill with a smile. The Japanese steakhouse was decorated beautifully with an array of floral patterns and shiny black counters speckled with flecks of gold. One wall had been painted to look like a grove of cherry blossoms; the brushstrokes were so lifelike, I could almost smell their sweet blooms.

Once we were settled into our seats, a waitress took our drink orders. I asked for a glass of plum wine and the other ladies in our party followed suit.

"That sounds really good," the tall leggy blonde, Melissa, I believed her name was, piped in from across the table. The other two women voiced their agreement.

A chef in a crisp white smock and tall white hat slid in behind the grill a few minutes later and greeted us warmly. We had a great time trying to catch food that he flipped expertly into the air with his spatula in our mouths. Dalton and I laughed at each other as each of us were pelted in the face with a piece of broccoli. Only a couple of our tablemates were able to catch anything in their mouths, but we all clapped enthusiastically when they did.

"So, what's your story?" Janie asked once our plates were full of fried rice, veggies, and an assortment of meats. I'd only learned her name because her husband liked to talk about her in the third person, bragging about all her accomplishments in the medical research field. Not that it wasn't sweet how proud he was of her, but it was getting old.

"Janie here discovered this."

"Janie learned how to perfect that."

His nasally voice was starting to grate on my nerves. I took a large gulp of wine to try and keep my irritation at bay before giving him the abbreviated version of my life. Dalton did the same, keeping it vague to avoid talking about Gianna and his recently broken engagement.

When dinner was over, we headed toward the last show the fire eaters were performing that evening. We watched in amazement as the young man dressed in nothing but a colorful pair of loose fitting, capri-length pants effortlessly handled the flames. He danced to the fast paced, upbeat music, easily balancing a burning stick in each hand. I found myself swaying to the music as I enjoyed the show. Dalton smiled down at me, amused by my enthusiasm, and wrapped his arm around my waist, pulling me into his side. I jumped back, shrinking away as the man held one stick up close to his face and sprayed liquid from his mouth, causing the flames to roar to life, increasing in size tenfold. Dalton chuckled and leaned into me, speaking directly into my ear, his voice low and full of gravel.

"Don't worry, I'll keep you safe." A shiver ran down my spine at the heady promise. It was a bit ridiculous how easily turned on I was by him, but with his fingers digging into my hip and his hot breath on my neck, there was no way I could remain unaffected. I couldn't wait to get out of there and escape back to our villa.

Fourteen

TAYLOR'S SWEET SCENT INVADED my senses and I groaned. My mind was hazy, and it was too dark to see her, but I could feel her. Visions from last night came flooding back into my brain and I happily replayed them, enjoying a rerun of the night's events.

When we finally stumbled back into our villa, our mouths fused together, the taste of plum wine on her lips, we were both ready to indulge in a little one-on-one time.

"I have an idea," Taylor whispered giddily against my mouth.

"What is it?" I asked eagerly.

"Follow me," she instructed, grabbing my hand and leading me to the back patio.

She walked over to the outdoor tub and turned the water on before slipping off her shoes. She started to take off her dress, but I stopped her. I'd waited all night to experience the pleasure of undressing her. Nothing was going to keep me from enjoying the task. I leaned down, gathered the material covering her legs, and bunched it in my hands as my lips met her neck. Her skin held a faint salty taste, a combination of sweat and the breeze off the sea. She groaned and her head fell to my shoulder.

I continued to lift her dress ever so slowly, drawing out the near agonizing anticipation. Pulling it over her head, I tossed it to the side and unhooked her bra. I spun her around to face me and knelt in front of her, my mouth even with her hips. She gasped as my teeth grazed her hip bone, trapping the tiny strap of her panties between them. I pulled it down, my fingers hooking into the other side, then kissed across her body until I found her center. Her fingers dug into my scalp when I planted a kiss there at the very top of her seam and my hands made quick work of removing the tiny scrap of material from her body.

Her lids were heavy with desire when I stood and brushed my thumb over her cheek, cupping her face. I pulled her to me, crashing my lips against hers and probing inside with my tongue. She let me in, meeting me thrust for thrust.

"Get in," I commanded. She stepped into the tub, turning the water off as she sank down into it. I got in and eased down beside her, our bodies angled toward each other. As soon as my ass hit the porcelain, she was on top of me, kissing me, her hands framing my face. She settled onto my lap, her knees straddling my hips. My dick was trapped between us, pressing against my stomach, or it would have been inside her. It was a good thing he was stuck where he was because he was unsheathed. As bad as I wanted her, as much as I would love to lift her hips and let her sink down onto me with no barriers between us, I couldn't. That would be completely irresponsible. Her brother was already going to be pissed about us hooking up. He'd be downright murderous if I got her pregnant.

As her hips thrusted and she rubbed against me, I damn near lost all self-control. She wanted a release and I was dying to give it to her. I reached between our bodies, putting a little space between us, and brought her to the edge with my fingers. She fell over it, digging her nails into my shoulders and moaning my name. Shit, that didn't make this any easier. I grabbed the little bottle of soap with the resort's logo on it and squirted some into my hand.

"Let me get cleaned up and we can have some *real* fun," I promised her, rubbing the lather into my skin.

She took the soap and did the same, washing up quickly. When she was finished with her body, she started working on mine. Her hands found my erection and stroked over it. I wouldn't be able to take much more before exploding. I grabbed her arms to still her hands and she frowned.

"If you don't stop, we're not going to make it to the good part," I informed her with a wolfish grin.

"Oh." Her features relaxed and she stood. Stepping out of the tub, she walked to the door and slid it open, not even bothering to dry off. Her wet, naked skin shimmered in the moonlight as beads of water dripped from her body. I opened the drain and scrambled out of the tub, following her inside.

I came up to her, gripping her hip and kissing her hard before throwing her onto the bed. She squealed in surprise and let out a giggle. I crawled over her body and my kiss swallowed the sound. Grabbing a condom from my drawer, I covered myself before sinking into her. I brought her to orgasm twice before succumbing to my own.

I blinked my eyes open, the memories of last night slowly fading away. My arm curled around Taylor and I pulled her closer to me. I was lying on my side with her back pressed to my front, and I was rock hard from thinking about last night. I slid my hand under her shirt, resting my palm against her stomach. She stirred and mumbled something unintelligible in her sleep but didn't wake. I let my hand travel up her breast, palming it like I had the morning I pretended I wasn't dreaming about her. She moaned and arched her back, rubbing her ass against my already aching erection. I sucked in a sharp breath and stilled my hand, gathering my composure for a moment. Once I was a little calmer, I began working my fingers over her nipple, playing with it until it was hard.

"Dalton," she breathed and arched her back again.

Fuck, I was about to lose it.

"Please," she begged. I lowered my hand to her waistband and slid inside her little sleep shorts. My fingers parted her, finding her already wet. She was definitely awake now and begging me to touch her. I was happy to oblige.

I grazed her clit with my fingers and she curled her hips forward, chasing a quick release, but I wanted to draw it out, to make her want it more with every passing second. With slow circles and gentle strokes, I continued to work her over with my fingers, trying to ignore my own need. She arched again and I cursed, my dick begging to be unleashed, but I powered through.

I reached lower, pushing my fingers inside, letting my thumb take over just above. She was soaked, her arousal dampening my hand. She was getting close. I could feel the little tremors in her core, her muscles tightening just before the release. She cried out loudly this time, her entire body convulsing.

As soon as my hand was out of her shorts, she rolled over, her eyes blazing.

"Please," she began. "Fuck me. Now," she demanded. I rolled on top of her and captured her mouth in a fiery, passionate kiss. I liked it when she got all bossy and demanding. It meant she needed this just as badly as I did. I rid her body of what little clothing she wore and whipped off my briefs before grabbing protection. I slipped easily inside her tight channel, the earth-shattering orgasm I'd given her removing most of the resistance.

I gave it to her fast and hard, relishing the way she screamed my name and begged for more. I'd been fairly gentle with her until now, but her body was getting used to my size, stretching and conforming to accommodate me. I didn't have to worry about being easy any longer. I didn't have to hold back. And I didn't. She was getting the full Dalton James experience this morning.

"How do you feel about paddle boarding?" I asked, running my fingers up and down Taylor's bare arm. We were cozied up in bed, still naked, enjoying a lazy morning.

"I've never done it before, but it looks like fun," she answered excitedly.

"I didn't have anything planned for today, but that's something you don't have to book in advance. Wanna try it out?"

She rolled onto her stomach and propped herself up on her elbows. "Umm, yes please!" she answered playfully, a huge grin splitting her face.

We ate breakfast and got ready, heading out the door an hour later. We would have been gone sooner, but she taunted me with that red, Brazilian-cut bikini, threatening to wear it paddle boarding. I pinned her to the bed and removed it from her body. Her eyes glowed red hot, not with fury, but with lust. She wanted me again. She did that on purpose so I'd take it off her. And she got her wish.

It took us a few tries to get the hang of the boards and maintain our balance. We both tipped over, splashing into the water once or twice, but we were both fast learners and in good shape. By the time we finished, I was regretting skipping out on the gym all week because my arms and shoulders burned from overexertion. Chagrined, I knew there was no excuse. We had full access to a state-of-the-art fitness center. I'd just been enjoying a different kind of physical activity.

We found lunch and then hopped on a boat tour just as it was about to leave the dock. We were pleasantly surprised by the glass bottom that allowed us to view the ocean life teeming under the surface. Taylor gushed over the coral reefs and colorful fish.

"Look, there's Nemo," she giggled, pointing to a little orange fish.

I remembered when the movie came out. She was crazy over it. Aiden and I met the year before in Mrs. Cranston's class and had been inseparable ever since. Aiden and Taylor's mom took the three of us, along with Taylor's best friend Avery to watch it at the theatre. I went along with Aiden, acting like I was too big for such a babyish movie, but I secretly liked it, too. That year, I gave Taylor a stuffed Nemo for her birthday. You would've thought I'd gotten her a pony by the way she acted. It made me wonder if she'd had a crush on me even then.

"Do you remember that stuffed Nemo toy I got you for your birthday?"

"Remember it?" she asked, pretending to be affronted. "I still have it."

"No you don't," I chuckled.

"Yes I do," she replied confidently.

"You're lying." I eyed her suspiciously.

"Scout's honor," she protested, holding up her fingers, making the gesture to go with her proclamation.

"Are you serious?" I was stunned and a little touched that she'd kept it all this time.

She nodded emphatically, a smile playing on her lips. I kissed her then, pulling her to me. She kept a stuffed animal I'd given her seventeen years ago. Gianna didn't even keep the custom-made bear I'd had delivered to her last Valentine's Day while I was out of town for work. Those two facts said a lot about these women and what they cherished.

I let thoughts of my ex fiancé float away. It was becoming easier and easier by the day. It made me wonder if I was truly still in love with her when she ended things. It wouldn't have been this easy to get over her if I was, would it? Or maybe I was just a piece of shit. I was engaged to another woman two weeks ago, and now I was sleeping with Taylor like Gianna never existed, like she never wore my ring on her hand to symbolize our love. What kind of person had I become? Was I turning into my father? He had no problem dropping the people he was supposed to love and care for like a bad habit.

I shook those thoughts away and moved back, putting a little distance between Taylor and me. She noted my movement and glanced at me curiously. I tried to school my features, but she could sense something was wrong.

"Are you alright?" she asked with a worried expression, reaching her hand out to rest on my knee. I flinched and pulled away from her, trying to pretend like I was just changing position. My head was reeling and I needed to get my thoughts in order, and her touch did nothing but muddle them.

"I'm fine. I'm just getting too hot." It was a lame cover, but it seemed to work. Her features relaxed and she returned her focus to the glimmering seascape below.

Once we were back on shore, we headed off in search of another adventure.

"What is that?" Taylor asked, her eyes lighting up as she pointed at something in the distance. I followed her gaze and it landed on a brightly colored object out at sea. I glanced down the beach to see if I could find where it came from and if there were more like it. Sure enough, there were several lined up and tied off about fifty yards away.

"That," I replied, pointing at the ones closer to us, "is a water trike."

"Oh my God, we have to try one out!" She started jogging toward them. Her energy was positive and contagious, and it brought the smile back to my face and eased my earlier trepidation. She marched straight to the rental kiosk and asked about renting one, pulling out her card before the lady behind the counter could answer her.

"Put that away," I chuckled behind her. "I'll get it."

"You don't have to do that. It was my idea."

"Taylor," I began, and she bit her lip and averted her gaze. I knew she wasn't working right now, and I didn't want her spending her own money on this. Besides, she was my guest. I didn't expect her to pick up the tab for anything.

"You don't have to pay for everything," she explained.

"Yes, I do," I assured her. "I asked you here. Last minute. And you graciously agreed to be my companion on what would have otherwise been a miserable trip. Please, just let me get it," I pleaded. Her shoulders slumped and I knew she would give in.

"Okay." She stepped aside so I could offer up my card.

We climbed onto one of the bright orange contraptions and set out to sea, peddling out into the crystal blue water. Taylor's elated laughter was infectious. The smile never fell from her face, and I found myself smiling in response. She was having the time of her life, and when that happened, her joy seeped into you. It invaded your entire being, your psyche, your heart, the pleasure center of your brain. You couldn't be unhappy when she was having that much fun.

When we finally returned to shore, we thanked the lady behind the counter and started the long walk back to our villa. We were both hot and tired, perspiration dampening our skin, so we stopped for ice cream on the way. It was a race to finish our two scoops before they melted and created a mess of sticky sweetness running down our hands. I tried not to watch as Taylor licked furiously over the dome of butter pecan, but I failed miserably. I loved her tongue and that hot mouth, and if I didn't stop looking at her, I was going to run into something, hard-on first.

Once back inside the villa, we changed into our swimsuits and reapplied sunscreen before heading out to the beach. This was our last full day here and we wanted to enjoy the sand and sun a little longer. We would only have tomorrow morning to frolic on the beach before we had to check out and head to the airport for our flight home.

I was disappointed to be leaving so soon. It felt like we just got here, like our vacation didn't begin until Taylor and I finally gave in to our desire for one another. I wish I had known it would be like this. I would've taken more time off work, but as it was, I needed to be back in the office bright and early Monday morning. I hadn't wanted to get in late Sunday night, so I opted to only stay here six days instead of seven. Now that I had Taylor with me and our time was quickly dwindling, I wished I had more than six nights in paradise with her.

I had no idea what would happen once we got home. We couldn't just go back to the way things were. I didn't want that, and I imagined Taylor didn't, either. We'd need some time to figure out how we fit together once we were back in the real world, before we took the terrifying step of telling her brother and the rest of our friends and family.

My mind raced with all the possibilities and scenarios as we waded out into the water to cool off after our day spent in the sun enjoying every activity and adventure we could find. I pulled Taylor into my arms and kissed her gently, needing to feel connected, needing her comfort. My hands tangled in her hair as I deepened the kiss, angling my head to better seal my lips over hers. She moaned in response and I felt myself growing hard.

"I wish this beach was completely private," she said when we broke apart. My forehead rested against hers and I let my eyes drift open. Hers were still closed, her pretty pink lips glistening from my kiss. "There's so much I want to do to you, right here, right now."

Her hands slid down my front, her fingers hooking into my waistband. I sucked in a breath, every abdominal muscle tightening with her touch. Damn, this woman knew how to get my engine revving.

My fingers curled into her hip when her hand slipped inside. We were in waist deep water, but it was clear enough that anyone who looked hard enough would be able to see what she was doing. I just couldn't make myself care enough to stop her. She licked her lips like she wanted a taste and I was dying to let her have it. Her dainty hand wrapped around my cock and immediately, she began to stroke me. She would be the death of me, but at least I would die a happy man.

"Taylor," I growled in warning. The corners of her lips tipped up in a devious grin. I loved this naughty side of her, loved that she wasn't afraid to let loose and let our passion take over. Dierks Bentley's "Somewhere On A Beach" began to play in my mind. If our trip had an anthem, it would be that. I was sure Gianna thought I was still heartbroken and moping over her. She texted me on Saturday, the day we were supposed to be wed to let me know she was thinking of me and hoped I was doing okay. I nearly threw my cell phone across the room.

Oddly enough, thinking of her now barely caused a stirring of emotion. I was focused solely on the woman in front of me with her hands all over my body. This trip was ten times more fun with Taylor than it would have been otherwise. We connected in a way I hadn't experienced before. And the sex… it was explosive. All those years of pent-up yearning and frustration built up like a powder keg, and our first kiss became a lit match.

Finally, I couldn't take it anymore and pulled her hand out of my shorts, scooping her up and carrying her out of the water. She wrapped her legs around my waist like it was instinctual, like our bodies fit together just like this and there was no other way to be held.

When I dropped her onto the bed, she leaned up on her elbows and her hooded eyes scanned down my body, stopping at the tented material just below my waist. I crawled over her and she dropped back onto the bed. My mouth fused with hers, muffling her moans as I pressed my erection against her center. We spent the rest of the afternoon exploring and appreciating each other's bodies as I wished for just a little more time with her before heading back home.

Fifteen

Taylor

"**WHAT MADE YOU DECIDE** to take a break from school?" Dalton and I were lying tangled in the sheets, his fingers running softly up and down my arm. My relaxed and sated body instantly tensed with his question. I'd been able to brush everyone else off when they asked, giving them some line about being burnt out and needing a break, but the truth was far more shameful. I'd hoped never to have to confess my sins to anyone else. It was bad enough the dean and Vice President of the university knew. I didn't need my friends and family finding out what a horrible human being I'd been. But the secret was eating me up inside. I needed a confessional. I needed to bare my soul and be absolved of my sins, but I couldn't bear to see the disgust in Dalton's eyes when he learned what I'd done.

A tear slipped down my cheek and before I could swipe it away, he cupped my face, forcing me to look at him.

"Taylor, what's wrong? Did something happen?"

His voice was so sincere, his tone laced with concern, that it broke my resolve to take this secret to the grave.

"I got in trouble," I sobbed, the tight knot of guilt that had settled in my chest a month ago starting to unravel. I'd let myself forget for a little while. I allowed myself to get lulled into a false sense of hope and innocence while Dalton and I were enjoying our little slice of paradise, but I could no longer bury my head in the sand, pretending I hadn't done something unforgivable.

"Tell me what happened," he urged gently, stroking his thumb over my cheek.

It took a few shuddering breaths to regain my composure and speak without my voice cracking. "You can't tell anybody," I pleaded. "Not my parents or my brother. They don't know. They *can't* know." I whispered the last part, shame flooding my entire being. They would never look at me the same again. Dalton probably wouldn't either, but if we were going to continue with this— whatever *this* was— when we got home, he had a right to know, didn't he? I wanted my sordid past to remain a secret, but it was eating me up inside and I needed to let it out. Would it free me or bind me even tighter in shame and regret?

"I slept with my professor." My voice was barely audible, the guilt tightening my throat, my airway nearly closing in on me. "My *married* professor," I elaborated. Dalton sucked in a breath and his body tensed.

Oh, shit. What have I done? He was going to think I was a terrible person. I had to tell him the rest. He needed to know I hadn't been aware of Jason's wife, or…

"I didn't know he was married." My words came out in a rush. "He never wore a ring, never talked about her, never let on that he was attached in any way to another woman." I closed my eyes against the disappointment and disapproval I knew must be written across his face. Would he ever be able to look at me the same after this?

"Start from the beginning," he said gently, brushing the hair from my face.

I took a deep breath. "Last fall, I took one of his classes. We hit it off instantly. He was funny and charming, and very attractive."

My stomach churned at how readily I'd lusted after him. He was tall and handsome, young to be a tenured professor, but also incredibly intelligent. He had messy brown hair and bright blue eyes framed by stylish, modern glasses. He had that sexy nerd vibe going for him that I found irresistible. When he'd roll his sleeves up during a lecture, his toned forearms would flex and I'd find myself wondering what he looked like under that perfectly buttoned up dress shirt. He was obviously very fit, but he didn't show it off. His clothes weren't too form fitting. He was unassuming, which only added to the allure.

"He asked me to stay after class one day to talk about one of my assignments. I was nervous, thinking I had messed it up and gotten a poor grade. I was pleasantly surprised when he told me how well I'd done." Dalton's hold on me tightened, but he remained silent. His tension was palpable, thickening the air around us. It suddenly felt hard to breathe, but I continued as best I could, pushing through the pressure in my chest.

"We struck up a friendship and he continually praised my work. If I got something wrong, he'd offer to go over it with me after class. One afternoon, he asked me to stop by during office hours because he'd left our assignments on his desk. When I finished my last class for the day, I raced across campus to catch him before he left. We started talking about the assignment, and he gave me some pointers on how to improve my work. The conversation flowed easily and before I knew it, we'd been in there nearly two hours. He was sitting in the chair next to me and we were talking like old friends instead of student and teacher. Of course, I had a huge crush on him, so it took me a long time to loosen up, but he eventually put me at ease."

Looking back, I knew I was an easy target. I fell right into his trap. He knew he made my heart flutter every time he walked into the lecture hall and stood behind the podium. I sat in the front row, just off to the right so I could be closer to him. I watched and listened with rapt attention during every class, and he took notice.

"When he walked me to the door, his hand stalled on the doorknob." I closed my eyes and wished the next part had never happened. He'd said my name, his voice low and husky. When I looked into his eyes, I could see the desire shining behind his lenses, his blue eyes burning even brighter. Our bodies leaned into each other and he closed the final gap between us. "We kissed," I said simply. Dalton didn't need to know the details. He didn't need to know how Jason had gripped my waist and pressed me against the wall beside the door. He didn't need to know that he tasted like coffee and French vanilla creamer, or that his hard body pressed against mine had me panting against his lips.

"He apologized and said he shouldn't have done that because he was my teacher and it wasn't fair to me." Little did I know just how right he was about that. "Nothing else happened for a couple weeks, and then he asked if I'd ever consider becoming a teaching assistant for one of his lower level classes. I jumped at the opportunity. He helped me with the application, and I started sitting in on one of his freshman classes shortly after. We spent a lot of time in his office going over lesson plans and grading tests. I was a little disappointed he didn't try to kiss me again, but by then, I'd signed up for the next semester's classes and knew I would have him again." I cringed at how obsessed I became. I wanted to be close to him, and even though there was another teacher who offered the same class, I coveted a spot in his.

"We were there late one night grading tests when he confessed that he wished I'd taken the other teacher's class instead of his. I couldn't believe he said that. My feelings were hurt because I felt like we got along great and I really liked him. But then he told me that he'd been counting down the days until he was no longer my teacher because it was a conflict of interest to date me." I swallowed past the bile rising in my throat. The next part solidified my position as an easily manipulated, naive airhead. I practically tackled him when he said that.

"That was the first time we hooked up." I looked down, focusing on a thread poking out from the sheet I was playing with to avoid Dalton's gaze. He cursed under his breath and the sound made tears well in my eyes again.

Jason wanted me and I readily granted his wish. I let him fuck me on his desk, basking in the taboo nature of our tryst. It was exhilarating and a little dangerous. It was after hours and though no one else was there that late, there was still a slight risk of getting caught. If I'd known what the consequences would be, it wouldn't have been nearly as exciting.

"Our affair continued well into the next semester, and just before finals, it all came crashing down." I took several deep breaths, needing to fill my lungs with oxygen before spilling the next part. It was by far the worst of it.

"I was sitting in the lecture hall one day while he was reviewing items for our final when the door creaked open and a woman walked in." I squeezed my eyes shut, trying to rid my mind of the memory of her, but it was forever burned into my brain. "She was stunning. Long blonde hair, sparkling blue eyes, and a designer handbag thrown over her shoulder. She came in smiling from ear to ear. Jason turned to see who'd waltzed in and interrupted his class and froze. 'Surprise!' she said and placed a hand on her protruding belly, rubbing it affectionately."

He dropped his dry erase marker, and to anyone else, it probably looked like he was just surprised and excited to see her, but I knew the truth. He was shitting his pants because his *very* pregnant wife had just walked into the classroom where his mistress was sitting front and center.

"It took me a moment to figure out what was going on. But when she stepped up to him and he pulled her in for a kiss, my world crumbled." Oohs and ahhs echoed through the room, but I felt like I was going to throw up. "I was devastated, so I grabbed my things and bolted. That move raised suspicion among some of my classmates, or maybe it solidified it. The next week I was having a meeting with the dean to discuss my future at the university."

"Wait a minute," Dalton said, raising up onto his elbow and staring down at me. "Why would *your* future at the university be called into question?"

"Because I had a sexual relationship with a professor," I responded slowly, confused by his question. Student-professor relationships were strictly forbidden, and I'd broken the rules.

"But you're not in a position of power. *He* is. If anybody's future at the university should be in jeopardy, it's his," he seethed, ire burning like a flame in his deep chocolate eyes.

"He's on probation and not allowed to teach again until fall semester. They required him to take leave over the summer."

Worked out perfect for him, really. His wife would be giving birth and his adulterous ass would get to spend the next three months at home with them. Meanwhile, I'd gotten off-course on my track to early graduation because of this.

"They requested I sit the summer session out and resume classes in the fall. I was just grateful they let me complete finals and didn't kick me out of school. My parents would have killed me. They had a proctor take over for Jason's classes that week so we wouldn't have any contact."

There were lots of murmurings over *that* and I caught several of my classmates giving me the side eye. They knew. Anyone who'd been paying attention all semester must've known what was going on, and my reaction to seeing him with his wife only solidified their suspicions.

"Taylor," he gritted out, raising his hand to his forehead and pinching his brows together, "they can't do that."

"Do what?"

"Kick you out of school for that."

"What are you talking about? I slept with my *married* professor."

"That doesn't matter. He was your superior. He had the power to pass or fail you; you had no such power over him. Sleeping with a student puts *his* future at stake, not yours. It should be written in your university's handbook."

"Then why did they question me so extensively? They made it seem like I did something worthy of expulsion."

ASHLEY CADE

"I don't know, but they were wrong. And that's intimidation. You need to hire a lawyer."

I bristled at his suggestion. I just wanted this to go away. I never wanted to see Jason again, and I certainly never wanted to be in that seat across from the dean again.

"Has he contacted you since?"

"He texted me to say he was sorry and that he never meant to hurt me." I rolled my eyes. What a crock of shit. He was just sorry he got caught. "He went on to say that he and his wife were having problems when everything started and the stress of becoming a father had gotten to him."

Dalton's jaw tightened and I feared it would snap in half. His own father bailed on him and his mom early on, claiming it was too much. He wasn't cut out to be a father, and Dalton was the one who suffered for it. At least he had my dad. Anything our dad did with Aiden, he did with Dalton, too. I was pretty sure he even gave him the birds and bees talk so his poor mom wouldn't have to.

"None of this is your fault. You know that, right?" He said it with so much conviction, I almost believed him.

"I didn't know he was married. I didn't know he was about to have a baby. But I knew I shouldn't have pursued a relationship with him and knew I shouldn't have slept with him. So yeah, that part's on me."

"I'm not saying sleeping with your professor wasn't a mistake-" I winced at his words, but he continued, "but you did nothing to deserve the way they treated you. They never should have held your education over your head. That can't go unanswered for."

His ire was oddly comforting. I reached up and cupped his face, reveling in the feel of his stubble against my palm.

"Thank you."

His features softened, his furrowed brow relaxing a bit. "For what?"

"For having my back," I replied. "And for not making me feel more ashamed than I already do," I added candidly.

"You have nothing to be ashamed of. You didn't make him cheat on his wife. He did that all on his own."

I rose up and brushed my lips against his, seeking out more of his strong, steadfast comfort.

We laid there for a little while longer, letting the shock of my confession wither away. His words made me feel human again, not like the evil seductress I'd made myself out to be in my own mind. He was right. I hadn't known the gravity of our mistake, or how negatively our affair would affect others, but Jason did. And he still pursued me. What a piece of work.

When it was time to get ready for dinner, we took turns using the shower, washing the sand and saltwater from our bodies. When I emerged from the bathroom, Dalton had changed the sheets and was making the bed.

"There was sand everywhere," he explained, tucking the last loose edge into place. The corner of his mouth turned up in a suggestive, crooked grin and I yearned to kiss it off his face.

There was a huge beach party happening tonight after the sun went down, and Dalton and I planned to celebrate our final night on the island. First, we had dinner reservations at the most popular restaurant within the resort. We splurged on filet mignon, lobster tails, and sangria. Our bellies were full and our hearts light when we headed toward the beach. His hand found mine and he laced our fingers together. I snuggled closer into his side, wrapping my free hand around his elbow.

The party was in full swing when we got there. Everybody had drinks in their hands and were enjoying the live entertainment. Dalton and I went to the bar and I ordered more sangria. We danced and laughed, partying with strangers and new friends. The night was magical. The breeze off the ocean kept us cool as the alcohol warmed our veins. Dalton only drank a couple beers, but he made sure my glass never ran dry.

As midnight neared, we decided to call it a night. We wanted to get up early enough to enjoy the ocean with its gentle waves and crystal blue waters one last time before leaving tomorrow afternoon.

Walking back to the villa barefoot along the beach, letting the waves wash over our feet, I thought back on our week, grasping onto every memory we'd made and holding tightly to each of them. I wasn't sure what would happen when we got home, and I didn't want to assume this would continue outside of this beautiful bubble enclosed within the resort. I hoped it would, but if all I had were these memories, I would hold onto them and cherish them forever.

Sixteen

WE WALKED INSIDE THE villa just as the clock rolled over into a new day. I couldn't wait another minute to have Taylor in my arms and her mouth on mine. Her lips parted on a gasp when I wrapped my arms around her waist and pulled her body flush against me. I leaned in, fusing my lips over hers and our tongues met, tangling in a slow dance of seduction.

She tasted like sangria, and suddenly Blake Shelton's voice echoed in my mind as we stumbled toward the bedroom, tugging at each other's clothes. She was tipsy and I was buzzed. We were clumsy but still alert enough to have some fun.

"Let's go down to the beach," she spoke against my mouth as she rid me of my belt.

I pulled back, catching the mischievous glint in her eye. "Seriously?" I asked, intrigued and a little scared of what she'd be able to talk me into.

"Yeah, come on," she urged, pulling me by the hand. "Where's your sense of adventure?" she taunted.

Never one to back down from a challenge, I pulled my shirt off over my head and followed her out. She ran for the water, giggling as she stripped away her clothes, leaving a trail in the sand. I threw caution to the wind and stepped out of my shorts and boxer briefs, tossing them onto the lounger.

She was completely naked, the pale moonlight reflecting off her skin. This was crazy. *We* were crazy. I knew it was late, but shit, I didn't want anybody to see us. Did security patrol this area at night? What the hell would we do if somebody came walking up the beach?

"What are you waiting for?" she yelled over the waves and I winced, hoping nobody heard her. I jogged down into the water, meeting her where the ocean lapped at our thighs. She attacked my mouth with fervor, sliding her hands around my neck and pressing her naked body to mine. I groaned and pulled her against me. We moved farther into the ocean, the water covering more of our exposed bodies. Her nipples grazed my chest and she shivered. I wanted them in my mouth. I wanted to taste the salt on her skin one last time.

When my head dipped to her chest, she threaded her hands in my hair, clutching me to her. My name fell from her lips on a whisper. I released her nipple and picked her up, carrying her deeper until the water concealed her chest. My cock slid against her hot, wet center and I instinctively flexed my hips. She lifted up, meeting my thrust as the head rubbed against her clit. A few more times and our rhythm became out of sync, and suddenly I thrusted inside her. She gasped and we both stilled. I was buried deep, Taylor's body clenching tightly around me.

"Taylor," I bit out, a little breathless. She felt fucking amazing. It took every ounce of strength in my body not to start pumping into her.

"Dalton!" she cried and rocked her hips.

I needed to stop this, but instead I gripped her hips and guided her up and down my length. "Fuck," I hissed, holding back my impending release. She kissed me hard, her arms braced on my shoulders. "We have to stop," I warned her. "I'm not wearing a condom."

"Shit," she breathed. "We have to get one." The moment I eased her off my cock was the saddest moment of my life. She unwound her legs from behind my hips and I placed her back on her feet. The water was nearly over her head, so I scooped her up and carried her back, leaving our clothes discarded on the sand. Rinsing my feet and lower legs as best as I could, I walked to the bed, laying her on top of the covers. The look in her eyes gave me pause for a moment. They shined with affection and something else I was afraid of. *Love.*

Taylor had been crushing on me for years, but this trip changed everything. This went beyond teenage infatuation and physical attraction. She cared for me. She may have even been in love with me. And that was the scariest thing on earth. Could I handle the responsibility of being the man she loved? She deserved so much. A man who would dote on her and make her his top priority. A man who loved her with the same ferocity with which she loved. A man who wasn't hiding out in a foreign country after being stood up by the person he thought he'd spend the rest of his life with. She deserved more than I could give her right now, but damn if I didn't want to try.

I pushed those thoughts aside as she drank me in, her hazel eyes darkening with desire. I almost sank back into her embrace and her tight warmth, but then I remembered why we came inside in the first place. Condoms.

Retrieving a packet from the box hidden inside the nightstand, I returned to the bed. When I tore open the foil, Taylor held her hands up, stopping me from rolling it on. I tilted my head, watching curiously to see what she would do next. She scooted to the edge of the bed and wrapped her dainty fingers around my length. When she licked her lips, I nearly fainted with anticipation. My head fell back as her wet lips slid over my crown and down my shaft.

"Mmm," she moaned, and the vibration sent a jolt of pleasure down my length, landing squarely in my balls. She made soft little noises like she enjoyed the taste and each one nearly undid me. When she finally let go of me with a loud pop, I was so close to coming, I had to take a moment to calm myself down.

I finally put the condom on and hovered above her. She placed her soft hands on my chest and slowly slid them down my torso, gripping me and guiding me to her entrance when she reached my arousal. My eyes closed and my head fell to her shoulder when I slid inside. She felt like heaven to a dying man.

I rocked into her, reaching between us to find her clit, knowing she'd go off like a rocket within seconds. She shattered apart quickly, crying out my name. I wrapped my hand around the nape of her neck and lifted until she was straddling me as I sat up. Her knees bracketed my hips, leaving her throat exposed and even with my mouth. My lips found her pulse, trailing kisses across her jaw and up her chin until they landed on hers. She found her second release, and mine followed shortly behind.

Leaving this place was bittersweet.

Wait, no. It was just bitter. I wasn't ready to go. I sure as hell wasn't ready to face everyone back at home. I couldn't stand their pitiful glances and words of encouragement. One would think the expression "there are plenty of fish in the sea" was played out by now, but no. People still used it. Besides, I wasn't looking for another fish. But Taylor had fallen right into my lap.

When I got on that plane last weekend, I had no intention of finding anything serious with someone new. My plan was to hit the beach and the bars, and if I found someone I vibed with, I'd consider hooking up with no expectations or emotions involved. Just pure, physical attraction and release.

I didn't expect Taylor's presence to affect me so explosively. I thought we'd do our own thing, aside from the activities I'd already booked, and simply come back to the same place to sleep. Most nights, at least. But that hadn't been the case. She had my undivided attention from the moment we set foot on this island, maybe even before then. Hell, I gave up my chance at a little mile-high action because of her. Taylor snuck up on me and I hadn't been ready to ward off her attack. She came at me with her adorable, endearing personality and subtle sensuality, leaving me positively defenseless. I wasn't sure where we'd go from there, but I was willing to find out.

I held her hand as we approached the gate, afraid that if I let go, I'd wake up and realize this was all a dream, that we hadn't spent the last six days having the time of our lives. She settled in next to me in our first-class seats and I placed my hand on her knee, giving it a squeeze. I wanted to touch her at all times, if for no other reason than to absorb the comfort her body provided.

"Ready to go home?" I was sure I already knew the answer, but I wanted to hear it from her own lips.

"No," she pouted and laid her head on my shoulder. She'd all but expressed that much when we were on the beach that morning, enjoying our last hoorah before departing our own little private paradise.

"I'll miss this," she said as I pulled her to me, her bikini-clad body tempting me to lift her out of the water and return her to the bed that would no longer be ours in a couple hours.

"Me, too," I confessed against her lips. Our kiss was deep and desperate. We were two lovers who felt as though we were running out of time. It wasn't like we wouldn't continue seeing each other once we got home, but we knew it wouldn't be like this. We'd have to go back to our regular lives, tedious obligations, and normal schedules. There would be days we couldn't see each other and would probably barely talk. We wouldn't have the luxury of having dinner together every evening or taking a stroll through the streets holding hands. Things would change. I just hoped we wouldn't.

Aiden was waiting for us when we landed. Taylor ran to him, rolling her luggage behind her. She was moving so fast it tipped over and threw her off balance. She just laughed and picked it up, righting it as Aiden closed the distance between them. He pulled her into a bear hug and her feet came off the ground. He released her and eased her back onto her feet as I stepped up beside him, careful not to get too close to Taylor lest I seem overly familiar with her.

"Man, you guys have nice tans," he complimented. "Did you do anything other than lay on the beach the whole time?"

I nearly choked, swallowing hard past the guilt clogging my throat. I didn't think it would be this hard to face him after giving in to the temptation that was his little sister, but the remorse was starting to creep in. Taylor glanced at me, but I wouldn't meet her gaze. I wasn't ready to confess, and I wouldn't allow him to glean any information on my betrayal from my expression.

"There was a lot to do at the resort," I offered with an easy smile, hoping he couldn't tell I wasn't being completely forthcoming. "We went scuba diving and paddle boarding, went to a dolphin encounter, and rode in a boat with a glass bottom." I let my voice trail off and my eyes drifted to Taylor, silently encouraging her to add to the conversation. I planned to tell Aiden about us eventually, but not here in the middle of the airport in front of all these people.

"The water trike was my favorite," she gushed, picking up on the direction I was steering the conversation. "And oh, my goodness, the food!" she exalted. "It was delicious."

Aiden watched her, taking in her excitement before letting his gaze flit back to me. He studied me for a long second before returning his focus to her.

"What else?" he asked.

He's probing. Why? Does he suspect something? Did he think there was a chance something would blossom between us when he suggested I take her?

"Oh, there was a sunset cruise," Taylor added. "It was amazing." I couldn't agree with her more. It had been fun to tease her, to slip my hand up her thigh and beneath her dress just to hear her breath hitch. But I couldn't tell him that. "And we got massages on the beach."

Shit. Those last two items sounded like something a couple would do. We hadn't even hooked up yet when we had the massage, but mentioning that along with the cruise sounded like we were lovers returning from our honeymoon. The irony was not lost on me that I was supposed to be doing just that, but not with the woman standing beside me.

"Sounds like you guys had a great time," Aiden offered, taking Taylor's suitcase from her. "I figured you two would be tired and hungry, so I thought we'd have dinner and then I'll take you home." The last part was aimed at Taylor.

I had wondered why he was here. I didn't expect him to be waiting on us, but he'd known when our flight was supposed to land.

"That sounds great! I'm starving," Taylor moaned.

After agreeing to meet at our favorite Italian restaurant, Taylor left with Aiden and I headed to my car. Once we arrived and were seated at a small round table, we ordered three different pasta dishes, each of us sampling all of them like we used to do when we were kids. I tried not to look at Taylor too much, but I didn't want to seem like I was avoiding her and raise suspicion. Aiden was watching us closely, looking for any sign that our relationship had changed while we were gone. Or maybe that was my guilty conscience talking.

I didn't think it would be this hard to face him again, but my mind kept returning to that day by the pool when we were younger. He was so adamant that I stay away from Taylor. If he'd changed his mind about that, he would have said something, right? Or maybe since I'd been with Gianna the last three years, he just let it go, figuring nothing would ever happen between us because I was committed to someone else.

I found myself sweating and tugging at the collar of my shirt nervously. Would I be able to stand up to my best friend and tell him I hooked up with his baby sister and wanted to see where our relationship would go? Would I lose his friendship for disrespecting him and not honoring his wishes? I was dangerously close to hyperventilating and was afraid I would pass out if I didn't get some air.

"Excuse me," I said as calmly as I could and stood from the table. I hurried to the restroom, bursting through the door and bracing my hands against the sink. Turning on the faucet, I splashed cold water on my face. I couldn't look at myself in the mirror for fear I wouldn't like what I saw. Had I irrevocably destroyed my friendship with Aiden? Would he forgive me for what I'd done?

Once I collected myself, I returned to the table and found the Wesley siblings joking and laughing. The tension eased from my shoulders and jaw as I took my seat between them.

"You should have seen him!" Taylor guffawed, her gaze settling on me. "His arms went flailing in the air and he hit that water *hard*." She drew out the last word, exaggerating it for emphasis. She proceeded to regale Aiden with a dramatic retelling of our paddle boarding adventure, making my lack of balanced gracefulness the butt of her joke.

"I wasn't the only one," I reminded her with a grin, and she giggled at the memory. She'd had her fair share of dunks in the pale blue water.

"That's true," she admitted easily.

After dinner, we headed to our respective homes. I fought the urge to pull Taylor in for a kiss, knowing her brother would see and we'd have to explain ourselves. She opened the passenger-side door to Aiden's silver

Beemer and looked my way. She hesitated, glancing longingly for a moment before settling into the seat next to her brother. I watched their tail lights as they drove away, wondering when I'd get to see her again.

It would be a while.

I spent most of Sunday unpacking my suitcase and catching up on laundry. My day didn't start until after noon since I was so exhausted, I slept through three different alarms on my phone. When I finally rolled out of bed, I discovered a text from Taylor.

Taylor: I have a job interview Wednesday. Wish me luck.

Me: That was fast. How did you land an interview in the sixteen hours we've been home?

Taylor: Aiden knows the manager. He got me the interview last week while we were gone.

Aiden was doing everything he could to help his sister succeed. He was so protective of her. He would lose his shit if he knew what happened with her professor and the university. I was half tempted to tell him, then we could go down there and give them a piece of our minds; but Taylor confided in me, trusting me to keep her secret. She didn't want her family to know what happened, what she'd done. If her parents and brother found out, she would forever feel as though a red letter "A" was burned onto her chest.

Me: That's great! You're going to nail it.

Taylor: Thanks!

Silence stretched between us and I wondered what she was thinking. If she was in front of me right now, I wouldn't have to guess. She'd tell me, either with her words or by her expression. She was an open book, and quickly becoming my favorite read.

I set my phone down, thinking our conversation was over, but it chimed with an incoming text a minute later.

Taylor: My interview is downtown. Want to meet for lunch?

Jeez, was I going to have to wait until Wednesday to see her? I'd spent nearly every waking minute with her the past week, and sixteen hours was already too long to not see her, kiss her, or touch her. I wanted her here with me tonight. I wanted to ask her to come stay with me, but I knew I wouldn't get any sleep tonight with her in my bed, and my day back in the real world would start early tomorrow morning. Besides, her absence at home after a week away would raise too many questions. Ones we weren't ready to answer yet.

Me: I'd love to.

Taylor: Great, it's a date.

A date. With Taylor. I loved the idea of going on a date with her. I'd just have to figure out how to either tell Aiden about us before then, or avoid being seen out together. If he heard about us from someone else, he would most definitely murder me.

When my alarm went off Monday morning at six a.m., I slammed my hand down on my nightstand, patting around for my phone. I found the button to silence it and sat up, rubbing my eyes. I tossed and turned last night, missing the feel of Taylor's warm body snuggled against mine. Maybe I should have just asked her to come over and stay the night.

I showered and dressed in my blue pinstripe suit, leaving my house in plenty of time for my usual Monday morning stop. After picking up a coffee from my favorite little cafe, I headed into the office. Opening my email, I winced at how many were waiting in my inbox. While I tried to stay on top of them while I was gone, I'd gotten distracted too many times to count, finally giving up when Taylor and I started spending more time in the bedroom.

I spent an hour sending out replies and scribbling notes on my legal pad about things that would need my attention in the next few days and was tapping away on my keyboard when my boss barged into my office. His face was pinched and a little ashen, his tired eyes full of panic.

"Is everything alright?" I asked as he strode up to my desk.

"We have a problem."

His serious tone made my hackles rise. *Did I screw something up?* I'd been so distraught over my broken engagement during the week leading up to my trip, it was entirely possible that I'd made a major mistake and he was waiting until I got back to confront me.

"What's wrong?"

"There's an issue with our facility in Seattle, and Jim's out after his knee replacement." Jim was my counterpart on the West Coast, and if he couldn't take care of the issue in Seattle, they would send...

"I need you to fly out there." His request cut off my train of thought, confirming my fears. "I know you just got back, and I'm sorry to do this to you after..." his voice trailed off and his gaze shifted away from me, "everything," he concluded. "But we've gotta get ahead of this, and you're the only person I trust to take care of it."

His eyes pleaded with me and for a moment, it almost seemed as if I had a choice. But in reality, I didn't. Refusing him would jeopardize my career, and truthfully, I didn't have a good reason not to go. Wanting to stay close to Taylor didn't count. Even though I wasn't yet privy to the details of the West Coast disaster, I had a feeling I'd be gone for more than a few days. This felt big, like something that would have me on the opposite side of the country for at least a week, maybe longer.

"When do I need to leave?"

"Tonight," he replied.

"Tonight?" I asked, taken aback.

"Yes, the sooner the better. Take care of what you need to here, then head home to pack. I'll have your assistant book your flight and hotel."

Fuck. This was not how I'd planned on starting back to work. But there was nothing I could do about it except excel at my job. I needed to be proficient and get this situation under control so I could get back home as quickly as possible.

When I landed in Seattle several hours later, it was already dark and I was ready for a hot shower and a good night's sleep. I took my phone off airplane mode when I got into the car my assistant rented for me, and it immediately dinged with several text alerts. Thinking it would be Taylor, I glanced down and noticed not only a text from her, but three from Gianna. Dear Lord, what could she possibly want? Against my better judgement, I opened hers first.

Gianna: Hey Dalton. How are you?

When that text went unanswered, she sent another.

Gianna: I'd really like to catch up with you. Give me a call when you get this.

Was she insane? Catch up? She called off our wedding five days before we were supposed to be married! Why the hell would I want to talk to her? I scrolled down, curiosity my only incentive for wanting to read what came next.

Gianna: Look, I know I'm probably the last person you want to talk to, but it's really important that you call me back. There's something I need to discuss with you. Can you meet with me this week?

Hard pass. I didn't care what she needed to talk to me about. I had no desire to see her after everything she did to us.

I considered leaving her texts unanswered, but I knew how persistent she could be. If I didn't respond, she would call and text until she got something from me.

Dalton: Can't. I'm out of town for work.

Gianna: Didn't you just get back?

Of course she would know that. Someone told her I went on that trip without her. Did they also tell her

Taylor went with me? Did anyone else but Aiden know she was going? Maybe Taylor posted about it on social media and Gianna found it. That was probably why she was suddenly interested in talking to me. She found out I'd taken another woman on our honeymoon, someone she knew had been in my life for years, no less.

Me: Emergency in Seattle. Had to go.

I kept my responses brief, not wanting to encourage her. She would keep going if I gave her too much or not enough. I knew how she operated.

Gianna: When will you be back?

Me: No idea.

It was the truth. I didn't know what awaited me tomorrow morning or how long it would take to sort out the mess.

She sent me a string of emojis, mostly frowny faces and little yellow circles with a tear running down their faces. I suppressed the urge to roll my eyes. I could just see her pouting, the corners of her lips turned down in disappointment. She could pout better than any child I knew. It was a little ridiculous for a woman her age. At one time I found it endearing, but now I cringed just thinking about it. My phone chimed with another text message.

Gianna: Call me when you get back.

I didn't respond. I had no intention of contacting her when I got home. The only woman I wanted to talk to was Taylor, and I planned on going straight to her house the moment I got back.

Seventeen

Taylor

I'M FLYING TO SEATTLE tonight. **Work emergency. I don't know when I'll be back.**

That was what Dalton's text said yesterday evening. I hadn't heard from him all day and was getting worried. I certainly didn't expect him to jump on another plane and fly across the country. I supposed that was a risk you took working in the corporate world.

I responded by wishing him a safe flight. I wanted to add that I hoped he made it home soon, but I didn't want to sound clingy and desperate. I needed to be careful with Dalton. He was coming off a very serious, long-term relationship and I didn't want to spook him. If I got too attached and started acting like this was serious, he would run and I'd miss my chance with him. So even though I missed him like crazy and would give anything just to hear his voice, I had to play it cool. I couldn't let on how desperately I wanted to be with him.

I went to the salon and got a trim so my hair would look fresh and neat for my interview tomorrow. It was a hostess position at one of the high-end restaurants downtown. It wasn't Exeter where I'd planned to apply, but it was just as nice. If I did well as hostess and impressed the manager, there was a good chance I could move into a waitressing position, which came with the potential to earn substantial tips.

When I got home, I picked out my interview outfit and hung it on the back of my door so it would be ready for me to put on in the morning. Aiden peppered me with practice interview questions to help me prepare. He'd never worked as a server or in the food industry at all, but he claimed a lot of interview questions were pretty standard and if I could handle his, I could handle anyone's.

I went to bed early, hoping to be well rested in the morning, but just like the past two nights, I found it difficult to fall asleep without Dalton's strong arms cradling me. Not only that, but I'd gotten used to the sedating effects of my nightly release.

I woke up early, even though my interview wasn't until ten thirty. The drive would take about twenty minutes assuming there wasn't much traffic, but I didn't want to take any chances. Aiden had suggested getting there a little early to show them I could be prompt, so I allowed myself twice the amount of time I needed to drive into town and find a parking spot.

My hands shook with nerves as I climbed out of my car. I'd only ever had two other jobs in my life. In high school, I worked at the local dairy bar in the summer serving ice cream and hot dogs. I didn't even need to interview for that job since the owners were friends with my parents and had known me since kindergarten. My second job was a cashier at a hardware store my freshman and sophomore years of college. I only got that job because the manager stared at my tits during the entire interview. I ended up being a shitty cashier since I wasn't very good at standing in one place for very long. When it was slow, I'd get bored and wander off, leaving my lane unattended. I got in trouble more times than should have been allowed, but surprisingly never got fired. Guess I was lucky the manager was so fond of my rack.

When my class load became too much and my GPA started to suffer, my parents allowed me to quit and focus solely on school. I was given an allowance for gas and other necessities that my paychecks had covered, and they continued to pay for my insurance as they always had.

Even though they were well off, my parents expected my brother and me to earn what we had, and since I wouldn't be taking classes this summer, I was entering the workforce again. There was no laying around the house, being a lazy freeloader in the Wesley household. Not that I could do that anyway. I didn't do well with idle time. I never understood how my friend Avery could stand it. She went to school during the fall and spring semesters, then spent her summers hanging around her parents' house binge watching Netflix and lounging by their pool. Don't get me wrong, I partook of the poolside relaxation time every now and then, but she made a career out of it. She would be in for a rude awakening when she had to start supporting herself.

It was eighteen minutes past ten when I walked into the restaurant. There were a few workers scurrying around, serving brunch items and collecting orders. It took a few minutes for someone to notice me standing there and come to the desk.

"How many?" the young waitress asked breathlessly, pulling menus from beneath the counter.

"Oh, I'm not here to eat," I said as she consulted her computer screen. She paused and her eyes flicked to me. "I have an interview," I informed her quickly. She seemed very busy and I didn't want to waste any of her time.

"Oh!" she chirped, perking up a bit. Her back straightened and she smiled. "Follow me," she instructed, turning on her heel and leading me toward the back of the restaurant. We turned down a hallway with a couple doors on each side and she poked her head inside one, informing the occupant I was here.

"Go on in, hun." She gave me another friendly smile and waved me inside.

"Ms. Wesley," the lady behind the desk greeted me, standing from her chair. She reached out and I took her hand for a shake. "I'm Caroline, the manager here at Francesca's."

"Hi, Caroline. It's nice to meet you." *Start with a friendly greeting.* Check.

"Nice to meet you, too. Let's get started." She motioned for me to take the seat across from her. I lowered myself into the chair, keeping my back straight but my posture relaxed. *Stay calm and confident, but don't act like you have it in the bag.* Check. "Your brother said you were looking to start right away," she began. "That is, if this job is the right fit for you and you for it," she added.

"Yes." I fought against the habit of saying *um* and *uh* and cleared my throat. "I won't be taking any classes this summer, so my schedule is very flexible and I'm available to start at any time."

"Great! Let's talk about the position, then I'll give you a tour." Caroline gave me the rundown on the job before peppering me with questions regarding my work history and experience. She explained that I would start out as hostess, my shift varying depending on the schedule and staffing. I could start as early as eight a.m. or as late as two p.m. Eventually I'd be trained to work the floor as a server. I still wasn't sure how she knew my brother or why she was willing to give me this interview, but I was too grateful to question it.

"Come on," she instructed, standing from her seat. "I'll show you around." I followed her out of her office and into the kitchen. The sous chef was adding ingredients into a large pot on the gleaming industrial gas stove, stirring after each dash of pepper and pinch of herbs. Another chef was chopping vegetables for salads while a third flipped portions of steak and chicken on the grill.

"Everything but drinks are prepared back here and placed there," she said, motioning to the shelf where a few plates of food were lined up, waiting to be retrieved by the servers.

We weaved our way through the dining area that was quickly beginning to fill and stopped at the front where the current hostess was preparing to sit a new party that had just arrived. She grabbed a stack of menus and led a group of finely dressed, middle-aged women to a table. Caroline deftly showed me how to keep track of which tables were open, which were occupied, and the wait staff who were assigned to them.

"It won't take you long to learn the system," she offered with a smile. We returned to her office and took our seats again. "Any questions?" she asked, folding her hands over her desk. I assured her she'd been quite thorough and that I didn't have any at this time.

"As you probably noticed, our need for a hostess is pretty urgent. Our wait staff are trying to seat customers in the morning when it's not as busy, but they're spread too thin as it is. Our current hostesses come in at eleven thirty when traffic starts to pick up, but we really need coverage all day. If your references check out, I have no doubt that there will be a job offer coming your way soon." That was great news. We briefly discussed pay, and when she told me what some of the waiters and waitresses earned in tips, my jaw nearly hit the floor. "We'll be in touch." She ended on that note and stood from her chair to walk me out.

I stepped out into the bright, late morning sun and took a deep breath. I might have a job very soon and I couldn't wait to get started.

"You!" a disgruntled female voice growled in my direction. There was anger and accusation in that one simple word, drawing my attention to the sidewalk. I glanced up and looked around as people passed by me quickly.

My eyes landed on a stunning blonde woman in her early thirties. Her hair curled around her shoulder and she wore a flowy sundress with pink and yellow flowers. She was dressed differently and her hair was loose around her face, but I would recognize her anywhere.

Jason's wife. Holy shit! She was standing right there in front of me and she recognized me. How did she know who I was? Did he tell her?

She stomped toward me, her face awash with fury. She poked her perfectly manicured finger into my chest and I winced.

"*You're* the little floozy who seduced my husband," she accused.

My mouth fell open. Is *that* what she thought? Did she really just accuse me of being a homewrecker on a busy city sidewalk in the middle of the day? My face burned with humiliation and anger. This day had been going too well. I should've known something would go wrong.

"That's right," she sneered. "I've got your number."

Her disdain sobered me and I shut my mouth. I really didn't want to do this here with an enraged, hormonal woman ready to give birth at any moment, but it needed to be said. I wouldn't let her make me into the villain. No, that title was reserved for her bastard of a husband.

"Look, Mrs. Barret, I don't know what you've been told-"

"Oh, I didn't need to be *told* anything," she interrupted. "I saw you run out of that room when Jason kissed *me*," she said, pointing to herself, "his *wife*," she spat, reminding me of her station. "When he finally came clean about why he was on probation, I knew it was you."

"It's not what you think," I began, the need to explain myself growing by the second. It wouldn't completely absolve me from my sins, but at least she'd know I wasn't aware of his marital status when we started seeing each other.

She scoffed, staring down her nose at me. "Isn't that what they all say? He told me everything."

Lies, I'm sure. If she was this mad at me, then he'd definitely fed her a line of BS.

"Did he tell you that he never once mentioned you to me?" Her eyes widened fractionally, giving me the answer she wasn't willing to voice. "Or that he never wore his ring on campus?" Her lips pinched into a flat line. "I had no idea he was married."

"Lies!" she croaked, her chin quivering. "He told me you knew and that you still went after him, that you cornered him in his office."

I flinched, stepping back as though she'd slapped me. "That lying son of a bitch," I mumbled to myself.

She watched me, her eyes wide like a scared cat. Her body vibrated with rage, but she was visibly uncomfortable and a little frightened. It was obvious she didn't typically confront people on the street. Here she was, ready to bring a child into the world, coming face-to-face with her husband's mistress. Anyone in her position would be unsettled, and considering the circumstances, she was keeping it together pretty well.

"I'm sorry," I began. "This is not a conversation I ever expected to have, and I really don't think we should be having it here," I said, gesturing around us with my open hand. "Can I buy you lunch or a coffee or something?"

Her mouth dropped open and her eyes widened in shock. "Why would you do that?"

"Because despite the fact I didn't know Jason was married, I still made a mistake and you got hurt because of it. I'd like the chance to clear the air with you, and honestly, I'm kind of afraid you're going to go into labor if we keep arguing in the street."

She surprised me by huffing out a laugh. "I'm kind of afraid of that, too," she admitted, rubbing a hand over her stomach.

She agreed to talk to me over lunch, so we walked a few doors down to a little bistro that served gourmet coffee and food. There was no way I could go back into Francesca's and risk being humiliated in front of my possible future employer and peers. We found a table tucked into a corner where we could have some privacy to hash things out.

"I can't believe I'm doing this," she said once we were settled.

"Same," I replied, just as surprised as she was. How the hell did we get here? I was about to have coffee with the wife of the man with whom I'd had a seven-month long affair. This was beyond awkward.

"I know I'm a stranger to you and you have no reason to trust me or believe anything I say," I began, jumping right in, "but I never once suspected Jason was married." She winced, pain flashing in her crystal blue eyes as she shifted uncomfortably in her chair. "I never saw a ring. There weren't any photos of you in his office." I would know. I'd spent plenty of time in there.

Her chin shook, but she kept the tears at bay. I wished I could take that last part back, knowing it hurt her even more than the sharp sting of his infidelity already had. He erased her from his life while he was on campus, pretending that he'd never vowed to honor and keep her in sickness and health, for better or worse. He portrayed himself as a bachelor, unbound to any woman. He certainly never let on that he was about to become a father.

"I would have never agreed to a relationship with him if I'd known," I assured her, projecting as much sincerity into my declaration as I could. I felt sick when I saw her and realized who and what she was to him. The fact that she was pregnant with his child made this even more unbearable. How could he do this to them?

A waiter came to take our orders before she could respond. We both glanced over the menus, making our selections quickly so he'd leave us to continue our conversation.

"Why should I believe you over him?" she asked. Her guard was back up and she eyed me with suspicion.

"I can't answer that for you," I stated simply. "He's your husband. He's the person you chose to spend your life with, which means you must love him and have great trust in him."

She swallowed hard and glanced away. There was a crack there, one that was growing by the second. She knew I was telling the truth. Woman's intuition was hard at work here, and she was fighting it valiantly. I continued before she had a chance to close that gap, wedging a fact that would be hard to swallow into that tiny sliver.

"But I have no reason to lie to you. I have nothing to gain from it. You're going to hate me either way, but I'm not the one who has to face you every day knowing that what I did was wrong. I'll walk out of here and quite possibly never see you again, but your husband is in a far more precarious position." He *would* have to face her again, potentially every day for the rest of his life, if he was lucky enough to keep her.

"Then why do you care?"

"I can't leave here without at least giving you my side of the story," I replied. "Because I think you deserve to know the truth." I didn't know her, but I knew she didn't deserve what he'd done. Cheating wasn't okay. Ever. If they were having problems like he claimed, he should've done everything in his power to work it out with her instead of stepping out with me. And I wouldn't let him continue to deceive her. I couldn't let him get away with the lies.

Her body sagged, her shoulders slumping in defeat. "How did it happen?" Her voice was so low, I barely heard her above the din of the lunch time rush. I winced and blanched, unsure if I could reveal to this already heartbroken woman how her husband had pursued me. It took me laying myself bare to Dalton to realize that was what happened, not the other way around. I'd put so much of the blame on myself that I didn't see how skillfully he'd orchestrated the events surrounding our affair.

"It started out just as any other relationship would. There was flirting and catching each other's eye when no one was looking. He pulled me aside after class one day to go over an assignment, telling me how well I'd done. After that, he gave me a lot of personalized attention, helping me with the things I struggled with and praising me when I did something right." She sat stoically, absorbing every word as though committing it to memory. "He asked me to stop by his office one evening because he'd forgotten to bring the assignments to class.

It was Thursday and he wanted to go over it before the weekend so I would have the correct answers for our test the following week."

Her jaw tightened and her nostrils flared. The ruse was obvious to her, but I'd been so enamored with him, I didn't realize what he was doing. Or maybe I did, but was so willing to go along with it that I simply didn't care. After all, I never suspected I was in danger of becoming the other woman, not just his forbidden love interest.

"That was the first time he kissed me," I confessed. Thinking about his lips on mine once made me giddy with excitement, my body flushing with heated anticipation. Now it just made me sad and a little nauseated. He kissed me, then probably went home to kiss her.

"Let me guess," she gritted out, her hands gripping the edge of the table so hard her knuckles turned white, "he asked you to become his teaching assistant so he could keep you close."

It wasn't a question. No, it was a statement of fact. Did he tell her how he'd seduced me?

"Yeah, how did you-"

"He's done it before," she spat, her face hardening. "A couple years ago, he started messing around with an undergrad and I caught them making out in his office." My eyes widened in surprise. This wasn't the first time he'd done something like this? She had seemed so willing to place all the blame on me, even though she knew he had a history of seducing his students.

"I wanted to believe he'd changed," she confessed, her voice cracking. "He promised." A single tear slipped down her cheek and she swiped at it angrily.

"I'm so sorry." I reached for her hand, but hesitated. I didn't even know her first name. I doubted she would welcome my touch or my comfort.

She sucked in a shuddering breath before continuing. "He claimed he never slept with her, but deep down I knew he was lying. I didn't want to believe it though, so I pretended I didn't. How could I be so stupid?"

"You're not stupid," I assured her. "You love him. He makes it very easy." There it was. The truth I hadn't wanted to face. The undeniable fact that made his betrayal even more excruciating. I'd fallen for him. He was so charming and attentive, it was hard not to love him. But that love fizzled and burned out, his infidelity extinguishing that flame like a fire hydrant to a candle.

"So did you," she affirmed, an array of emotions playing over her features. Sorrow, anger, heartbreak, jealousy.

"I did," I admitted. "But not anymore." My heart belonged to another.

Dalton.

He was like a ray of sunshine, illuminating my self-worth in my darkest of days. His invitation to paradise was my saving grace. That week I spent with him put the broken pieces of my soul together after another had shattered it.

"I still do," she confessed. "How pathetic is that?" My heart broke all over again for her.

"You are *not* pathetic," I declared. "He is your husband," I echoed my earlier statement. "You vowed to love him unconditionally and through any hardship, right?" She nodded her head. "So, you've held up your end of the bargain."

She wiped at her eyes again. I didn't know what it was like to be in her position, to be married to someone and love them so deeply, even though they betrayed you. I wouldn't judge her for continuing to love him, but I wouldn't pretend he deserved her forgiveness, either. Ultimately, that was her decision to make.

"It's okay to keep loving him. You probably always will. But you don't have to forgive him." Her expression morphed from defeated to stunned. "That part is totally up to you. Nobody else can make that decision for you."

"I have to," she choked out. "Our baby," she said, cradling her stomach.

"I understand." I reached out again, taking her hand this time. "You do what you think is best for you," I instructed, my eyes dropping, "and for your child."

Did I think she should leave his ass and take him for everything he had? Of course. But she needed to come to that conclusion on her own. If she decided to forgive him and give him another chance, I hoped he took it and cherished it. I hoped he became the best father and husband anyone could ask for. I just didn't have much faith in his ability to do so.

Her shoulders shook with silent sobs and I squeezed her hand, offering what little comfort I could. I couldn't imagine the pain she must be feeling. Jason was lucky to have someone love him so deeply. He was a damn fool who certainly didn't deserve her.

"Mrs. Barret, I-"

"Melody," she corrected. "Please, call me Melody."

"Okay," I agreed. She looked like a Melody, all poised and beautifully put together. "Melody, I hope that no matter what, you find happiness. You deserve better than the mess that's been heaped on you, and I'm truly sorry for my part in it."

"Thank you," she sniffled and wiped her eyes one last time. "And I'm sorry for attacking you like that," she added sheepishly, hanging her head in shame.

"It's okay. I honestly think anyone else would have clawed my eyes out."

She giggled, then broke into full-on laughter. I was relieved she found my joke funny. Someone had to lighten the mood around here.

"Ah, thank you. I needed that laugh. It's been far too long," she admitted, wiping at her eyes that were now watering from laughter. I was thankful they weren't tears of despair anymore.

Our lunch arrived shortly after, putting a hold on further conversation. We left that bistro with our bellies full and our hearts a little lighter.

"Thank you for that," Melody said, motioning to the building we just exited. "I needed to hear your side of the story and the brutal truth about my husband."

I nodded. "I'm sorry we had to meet this way. I think under different circumstances, you and I could have been friends."

"I think you're right." She smiled, and the look suited her far more than the sad, angry visage of a woman scorned.

"I'm Taylor, by the way. I don't think I properly introduced myself." I reached out and offered my hand.

"I don't think I gave you much of a chance," she replied, taking it.

We shook and parted ways. We may not have been friends, but at least we were no longer the enemies Jason turned us into.

Eighteen

I **TOSSED MY SUIT** jacket over the back of the chair and fell face first onto the bed. This was a nightmare. The situation in Seattle was a disaster. I didn't know if Jim had fucked up royally, or if the shit hit the fan because he left the place unattended. Either way, it had somehow turned into *my* mess and I was responsible for cleaning it up.

It was just after ten at night and I was ready to pass out. I'd spent the entire first day going through paperwork that had been grossly mishandled. It was obvious that whomever Jim left in charge wasn't doing their job. Eight hours into wading through the mounds of invoices, expense reports, and other ill-collected data, I was ready to fix the whole problem with a can of gasoline and a lit match. This was going to take forever. All I wanted was to see Taylor, but I wouldn't get my wish for probably two more weeks. All we had for now were a few text messages and the promise of a video chat when both of us were free.

The next day was much like the first. I called it quits around six thirty that evening and headed back to the hotel and hit the fitness center. I hadn't worked out since before my trip and I needed a way to alleviate all the stress from being out here when where I really wanted to be was wrapped up with Taylor in my sheets.

An hour and a half later, I could barely walk and my arms felt like Jell-O, but I was far more relaxed than I'd been in days. I went back to my room and ordered room service, catching up on emails while I waited. Not only did I have to take care of the current issue in Seattle, but I had to stay on top of the work I left at home. There was a lot my team could do without me being right on top of them, but it was still my job to manage them and make sure everything got done. After I concluded this fiasco, I planned to ask for a raise.

When my dinner finally arrived, I inhaled it. I wasn't accustomed to going so long without food, but after lunch, we'd worked up until the moment we left, and then I went straight to the gym.

With my stomach full, I was finally able to think more clearly. I wanted to talk to Taylor but had no idea what I'd done with my phone. I finally found it in the back of the pants I'd worn to work. I'd been so busy today, I hadn't taken the time to check it. When I pulled it out, there were a couple messages from her.

Taylor: Interview went great! Hope to hear something soon.

An hour later, she'd sent another text.

Taylor: You'll never believe who I just had lunch with. Call me when you get a chance.

I wasn't sure I liked the sound of that. Had she eaten with her brother? Did he know about us now? I double checked my phone. I had no missed calls or messages from him, so I doubted that was who she was talking about. Could it have been someone at the school? Maybe they came to their senses and stopped treating her like a damn criminal.

It was late and I wasn't sure she would still be up, so I fired off a quick text instead of calling just in case she was already asleep.

Me: Hey, sorry I haven't called. I just got in. It's a mess out here. You still up?

I waited several minutes, just staring at my phone, willing her to respond. I'd give anything to hear her voice right now. When I didn't hear from her after ten minutes, I hopped in the shower, leaving my phone on the sink so I'd hear it ring if she called. She didn't. Slipping beneath the plush comforter of my temporary bed, I fell right to sleep. I didn't even have time to set my alarm before drifting off.

Somehow, it still went off the next morning, my phone chirping annoyingly at me. It sounded wrong, not like my usual alarm. My eyes flew open and I reached for my cell. It was ringing, the number to the Seattle office flashing on my screen. Shit. It was past eight and I'd instructed everyone to be there by now. I jumped out of bed and ran to the bathroom, silencing the call. My teeth were brushed, my hair was combed and styled, and a clean suit decorated my body within five minutes. I called back to let them know I was on my way. It was technically the truth since I was speed walking down the hall as we spoke.

When I finally made it to the office, everyone was eagerly awaiting my arrival. I assigned them each a task and shut myself inside Jim's office. I had a call scheduled with him at nine. I needed his input on a few things and wanted to pick his brain to see if I could determine where the breakdown began.

An hour later, I'd finished off my second cup of coffee and had an idea of where things went wrong. Jim didn't want to point fingers at anybody, but it was clear his second-in-command was the problem. It sounded like Gary had always wanted more power and a chance to prove himself. He'd proven himself, alright, just not the way he hoped. Without Jim there to keep him in line, he had free reign over the projects Jim was overseeing and he nearly ran them into the ground. He would be lucky to keep his job after this.

Gary and I sat down and had a nice, long meeting where we went over everything that had gone wrong over the last four weeks. I asked him to take me through every single task and decision he'd made so we could form a plan of action, and I counseled him on his terrible management skills. He hadn't delegated appropriately and filed forms incorrectly. His desk and computer were a disorganized disaster. It would take us another whole day to deal with that mess.

We didn't break for lunch until two. I checked my phone and noticed Taylor had texted me back that morning.

Taylor: Hey, just got this. I went to bed early last night. Sounds like you've had a busy day.

Me: Very busy. Today is more of the same.
She responded back immediately.

Taylor: Oh no! Will you have to be out there long?

Me. Probably. I'm guessing a couple weeks.

Taylor: Can you talk?

Instead of responding, I called her. I was anxious to hear her voice and didn't want to wait another second. Plus, this was the only break I would get all day. She picked up on the second ring.

"Well, hey there, big shot," she answered in greeting and I smiled. I loved how her playful spirit instantly put me at ease.

"Hey," I replied, my mood lifting. "How are you?"

"I'm good. I have lots to tell you. I'm glad you called."

"Yeah, me too. I needed to hear your voice." *Oops. I didn't mean to say that out loud.* I heard a little gasp on the other end of the line and then nothing.

"Same here," she replied after a moment, her voice low and wistful.

She needed to hear my voice, too? Silence hung in the air between us. Why was this so awkward? I'd been inside her. My mouth and hands had explored every inch of her body. Put a few thousand miles between us, and suddenly we didn't know how to talk to each other. After several long seconds, I cleared my throat.

"So, what did you want to tell me?"

"Oh!" she chirped excitedly. "I got the job!"

"Congrats. That's awesome! You must've really impressed them to already be offered the job."

She snickered. "I think it's more like they were desperate to fill the position and I was readily available."

"Hey, don't sell yourself short. I'm sure they were able to see just how amazing you are." I pulled the phone away from my ear and smacked the edge of it into my forehead. Why the hell did I keep saying shit like that?

Because she is *amazing,* a little voice piped up from the back of my mind. Even so, I needed to lay off all the compliments and affectionate little declarations. Whatever this was between us needed to move slowly. Saying things like that to her made this more serious than I was willing to get at this point.

"I also, um," she began, stammering a bit. *Uh oh, this couldn't be good.* "Had lunch with Jason's wife." I made the mistake of taking a sip of my water while she was speaking and nearly choked on it, spitting it halfway across the room.

"You *what?*" I croaked between coughs.

"Are you okay?" she asked with concern.

"Yeah, go ahead." I collected myself, taking another drink of water to soothe my throat.

"I ran into her coming out of my interview. She recognized me and was pissed." She let out a little chuckle.

What on earth could she find funny about that? I wondered. She proceeded to relay the entire incident to me and the conversation that followed. The poor woman sounded broken but determined. While I felt terrible for her, I was relieved for Taylor's sake. Meeting with Jason's wife and having an open, insightful conversation with her seemed to lighten the burden of her guilt even more. I knew confiding in me helped and I'd been able to make her see she wasn't to blame for Jason being unfaithful, but having his wife's understanding and forgiveness did far more for her conscience than I ever could.

"I'm glad you ran into her, then."

"Me too. I hate to say this, but I hope she doesn't stay with him. He's a pig and she deserves so much better. But if she can find it in her heart to forgive him and he stops screwing around on her, I hope she can be happy with him again."

It amazed me how sweet and compassionate she could be. I thought Jason deserved to be kicked in the nuts and forced into celibacy for what he'd done to them. I knew first-hand what it felt like to have an unfaithful partner, to see them with someone else every time you closed your eyes. God, I could just imagine that man bun flopping around every time Gianna spread her legs for Antonio.

"Dalton, are you still there?"

"Yeah, sorry. I'm here."

How had I let thoughts of my ex-fiancé slip back into my mind while talking to Taylor? I was getting over her. Taylor was helping me forget about Gianna and how she'd torn my heart out. At least, she had been. While we were secluded on that island, she brought me back to life in more ways than one and made me forget how much Gianna hurt me. But Gianna's persistence over the last few days unnerved me, and all those old feelings for her kept trying to resurface. I worked to push them back down, but with every text and phone call, a little bit would break through the surface again. Every time her name flashed across my screen, a multitude of emotions came flooding back.

I was growing leery of my relationship with Taylor. We hadn't put a label on it, and I was in no hurry to, but we had something special. I just didn't know if either of us was ready for it. Her heartbreak was nearly as fresh as mine. Were we both in danger of being each other's rebound?

Taylor switched gears and told me a little about her new job. When I started to yawn, she giggled and offered to let me go. I apologized for yawning in her ear, but she assured me it was alright and gave me strict orders to get another cup of coffee. Before we hung up, I made sure she knew it would be late her time when I finished up and I'd probably wait until tomorrow to call her. Her time zone was three hours ahead of mine, and I didn't want to keep her up until midnight just so we could talk.

The next day ran a little more smoothly. It was Friday and everybody was ready for a break, including me. I would come into the office tomorrow and work solo, taking advantage of the solitude and lack of distractions and interruptions. I could get twice the work done and possibly be one day closer to going home.

Gianna was at it again, asking when I would be back in town. I was tempted to tell her to leave me alone, that I had no desire to see her now or in the future, but I just couldn't do it. I was worried something was terribly wrong since she was so insistent on telling me in person. My thoughts immediately went to her mother who'd had a cancer scare a couple years ago. She ended up having a total hysterectomy to ensure it wouldn't spread and had been given a clean bill of health at every check-up since. Had that changed? I hoped that wasn't it.

With that in mind, I shot back a quick text, my response softening.

Me: I'm hoping sometime next week. I'm going to work all day tomorrow to see if I can speed things along.

Gianna: Okay. Have a good day, D.

She was using my nickname again. She used to call me D all the time, but had stopped sometime in the last couple months. I didn't think anything of it at first, but looking back, that must have been when she started falling out of love with me.

The day passed quickly, and since we'd made a lot of progress, I accepted an invitation to join the rest of the team for drinks after work, leaving the office at a normal time for once. We enjoyed a couple rounds at a swanky uptown bar, and I was able to get to know some of them a little better. Gary, who'd been sulking since our meeting, finally loosened up and joined in the conversation.

At seven, I decided to finish off my last drink and head back to my room so I could get an early start in the morning. I called Taylor when I got in, catching her as she was heading home from work. It was her first day on the job and she sounded exhausted.

"After the first couple hours, I was on my own," she said, sounding overwhelmed but proud. She handled it well and received no complaints from anyone on shift tonight. We ended our call when she pulled up to her house and we promised to talk more tomorrow night.

Saturday came and went in a blur. I worked well into the evening, but I accomplished twice as much as I had any other day. Maybe I'd be home by mid-week, after all. I decided to find out Taylor's work schedule and surprise her, maybe convince her to spend the night with me. I couldn't wait.

There was a spring in my step as I walked through the hotel lobby. This disaster was coming to a close faster than I expected.

"Dalton." The familiar voice stopped me in my tracks and I turned, hoping I was mistaken. Gianna stood from one of the plush couches that peppered the lobby and smoothed out her dress before approaching. She walked slowly toward me as though she feared I would run if she made any sudden movements.

"What are you doing here?" I bit out, my shoulders going from relaxed to tense in a flash.

"I needed to see you." Her voice and eyes were full of pleading.

"So you just show up *here*? In Seattle?" I stood, disbelieving her gall as she took another wary step toward me. She was now within reach and I wanted to shake her. Why the hell did she fly all the way to Seattle?

"It's important."

"So important it couldn't wait until I got back?"

She nodded, her eyes wide and scared. Unease clenched my stomach. This couldn't be good.

"Come on." I walked to the bank of elevators and punched the up button. Whatever this was about, it was best to discuss it in my room and not in a crowded lobby with people milling about. She followed, her heels clicking against the marble floor. Each tap sent a bolt of anxiety through my body. I was nearly shaking with nervous energy by the time the doors slid closed.

I threw off my tie and jacket when we entered my room and turned to face her. She looked worried, like she knew I was going to throw her out as soon as she spilled the beans.

"What's this about, Gianna?" I asked, exasperated. She pulled something from her purse and approached me warily. *What the hell?* She handed me the square paper and I looked down. My heart dropped, sinking to the pit of my stomach like a lead balloon.

Nineteen

Taylor

I **CALLED DALTON WHEN** I got off work, hoping to spend the drive home talking to him again, but he didn't answer. All my texts and calls went unanswered the next day, too. I was starting to worry, thinking maybe something had happened to him. He could be hurt or lying in a hospital somewhere and nobody would even know. I considered asking Aiden if he'd heard from him, but then he'd want to know why I was asking. *Shit.* This wasn't good.

I paced my room and agonized over what to do. Maybe I'd try calling him one more time. But if he'd already seen all those missed calls from me, it might send him running for the hills. I finally settled on sending him another text.

Me: Hey, let me know you're okay. I'm about to have Aiden call you.

My phone dinged two minutes later. *About damn time.*

Dalton: Hey, sorry. I've been busy.

That's it? Two ignored calls and three missed texts and that's all I got? I huffed out my frustration. Why was he being so weird? I threw my phone down on the bed and headed for the shower. Now that I knew he was fine, I refused to stay glued to that thing any longer and decided to go about my business. I had to be at work at nine tomorrow morning, so I needed to get ready for bed anyway.

When I returned, I had a few messages. I opened my texting app and read them, then dropped the phone as if it had burned me. Shaking, I picked it back up, hoping I had just read them wrong.

Dalton: I think we need to put the brakes on this thing that's happening between us. It's too much too soon. I'm sorry.

My stomach clenched and my chest tightened. *No. No, no, no.* This couldn't be happening. I'd finally gotten my chance with him. It couldn't be over so soon. My eyes greedily searched out the next message, hoping he'd changed his mind.

Dalton: We're both coming off of bad breakups and neither of us is in a position to get involved with someone else so soon. I don't want us to rush into something we're not ready for. And I don't want us to be each other's rebounds.

I could agree with that last part, but he wasn't really my rebound. He was the one I'd been waiting for my whole life. It just took a few bad relationships and a trip to the Caribbean for us to find our way to each other.

Dalton: I still care about you and hope we can remain friends. But for now, we both need to take some time to get over everything that's happened. Maybe someday we can try this again.

I crumpled onto my bed, clutching my pillow to my chest. I had my shot with Dalton James and blew it. Tears slid down my cheeks. This couldn't be the end. I just needed to talk to him in person. He needed to see me, to be close to me so he could feel the chemistry between us and know that what was developing between us was real.

Me: Don't do this.

Me: We can take things slow. You know there's more between us than friendship. We can't just ignore that like we've been doing for years.

Dalton: I'm so sorry. I just need some time.

What was I supposed to say to that? *No, I won't give you time?* I couldn't do that. I would lose him forever. So, I texted back the only thing I could.

Me: Okay.

The rest of that week, I looked and felt like a zombie, just going through the motions without purpose or conscious thought. Work was the only distraction I had, and I was desperate for it. I even asked for more hours even though I already had overtime. I was able to stay late a couple evenings and help the servers while the other hostess was on duty. Mercifully, sleep came easily most nights since I worked myself into the ground every day. It was all I could do to shower before falling into bed.

The following Monday, I received an email from the university stating I could register for classes for fall semester. I found the codes for all the classes I needed and plugged them in, praying they were still open. Thankfully, I was able to get everything I needed. I double-checked to make sure Jason wasn't teaching any of them before hitting submit.

As the week went by, the fog lifted a bit and so did my spirits. It was my second week without Dalton, and although my heart still longed for him, I managed to function more like a normal human being. My class schedule was set for fall semester and I was doing well at my new job. My first paycheck was amazing because of all the hours I worked, plus I'd started earning tips. I was riding high going into the weekend, but Saturday morning, I crashed and burned.

I was updating the computer screen with available tables when the door opened and someone walked inside. The person was almost to the counter when I looked up. All the air left my lungs in a rush and I froze, staring up into the perfectly made-up face I'd hoped never to see again.

"Kayla," Gianna crooned in fake excitement. "It's *so* nice to see you again. I didn't know you worked here."

I shook myself from my state of stunned paralysis. "It's Taylor," I corrected gently. She knew that. She'd known me for three years. That was just her way of being a spiteful bitch. She must've known by now that Dalton took me on that trip, the one she was supposed to be on. Why she would care about it was beyond me. She was the crazy one who called off their wedding.

"Nice to see you too, Gianna." I plastered on a fake smile and reached for the menus. The door opened again, bringing with it a humid breeze and the sound of rain pelting the concrete outside. "How many are in your party?" I asked, peering down at the computer screen to check available tables.

When I looked up, I felt like I'd been punched in the gut. Dalton was standing next to her, his hand resting on the small of her back. He stiffened as his eyes locked with mine. Our gazes remained fixed on each other, both of us shocked at the sight of the other. I fought back a sob and swallowed hard.

This was why he ended things between us and hadn't talked to me in nearly two weeks? To get back together with *her*?

"Four," Gianna answered, drawing my attention back to her. I blinked up at her, my brain searching for meaning behind the word. "There are four in our party," she explained, put out by my confusion. "My parents are joining us." She turned her body into Dalton's and slid her arm around his, resting her hand possessively on his bicep. If it was possible, he tensed even more. The corner of his eye twitched and the muscles of his jaw flexed.

"Right." I grabbed four menus. I glanced past them, searching for two more people, but didn't notice anybody else. "Would you like to be seated, or would you prefer to wait on the rest of your party?" My voice shook as I fought back tears, but I'd be damned if I let either of them see how hurt I was, especially Dalton.

"You can seat us now." Gianna's tone was condescending. She'd always been a little aloof around me, but had never been outright hostile. That had obviously changed. Oh, she definitely knew about us. "I'm starving," she complained dramatically, her hand going to her stomach. The gesture was familiar. I'd seen someone else do that recently but couldn't place it. My mind must have still been foggy.

"Follow me," I instructed. I wouldn't look at Dalton, refused to meet his eye. If I did, I would lose my composure. I was slowly breaking and couldn't let them see it. I'd be a bigger mess than Melody was that day at the bistro.

My step faltered as I thought of her. The way she'd rubbed her protruding belly…

Oh, God. That was who Gianna reminded me of. The way she touched her stomach, like there was something in there to love and protect. I coughed to cover my sob. We were only a few feet away from their table. I wasn't going to make it. I was about to lose my shit right there in the middle of the restaurant. I sucked in a few deep breaths, doing everything I could to keep the tears at bay. I could do this. I *had* to do this. I wouldn't let him see me break.

I calmly set the four menus down on the four place settings and let my focus land on a point past Gianna's shoulder. "Your server will be with you shortly." I turned on my heel and walked away.

"Taylor." I jumped a bit at the sound of Dalton's voice calling my name, but my step never faltered and never slowed. I headed straight to Caroline's office.

"Taylor, what's wrong?" she asked when I stepped up to her desk. "You're pale as a ghost." She stood and came around to my side and placed the back of her hand on my forehead.

"I'm not feeling well. I think I need to go home." It was the truth. I felt my heart cracking open, my insides turning to dust and floating away. There was nothing left of it now.

"Of course. Go," she urged. "Do you need someone to drive you?"

"No." There was no way I could wait for someone to take me home. I had to leave now. "I'll be fine," I assured her before stiffly walking out the door. I rushed out of there, not daring to glance into the dining area for fear of seeing Dalton or Gianna. Once I was safely inside the confines of my car, the flood gates opened and all my pain came pouring out.

When I first saw him standing there next to her, I couldn't figure out how he could have gone back. After everything she did to him, how could he choose her? But if she was pregnant with his child, he wouldn't turn his back on her. He'd try to make it work for the kid's sake. He would never put someone through what his father put him and his mother through. His biggest fear had always been that he'd turn out like him.

But hell, that didn't mean he had to jump back into a relationship with Gianna. There were plenty of people who made co-parenting work. Dalton would make a wonderful father, regardless of his relationship with the mother. Yet, he chose her.

I sat there for a long time, tears leaking from my eyes like the incessant rain that poured over my car. My top was soaked, but I wasn't sure which source the water had come from, my eyes or the sky. I pushed damp tendrils of hair from my face and wiped my nose. It was time to head home and forget I'd ever loved Dalton James.

When I got home, I went straight to bed, burrowing under the covers before crying myself to sleep. That was where Aiden found me hours later when he came home.

"What the hell?" he barked from the doorway. "Why aren't you at work? Did you quit already?" he questioned angrily, stalking toward my bed. I rolled over and he flinched at my appearance.

He let out a low curse as he sank onto the edge of my bed, taking in the sight in front of him. I could feel how puffy my face was, my eyes nearly swollen shut from crying, my hair matted to my cheek from the tears. "What happened?"

I shouldn't have told him. He didn't need to find out this way. I didn't have any right to drive a wedge between my big brother and his best friend, but I had to tell someone, and Aiden was looking at me like he was seriously considering calling a priest to give me my last rites.

So I gave my confession. I told my big brother everything.

Later that evening, I was curled up on the couch with a bowl of ice cream, watching a movie with Aiden. He'd cancelled his Saturday night plans to stay home with me. Our parents were out of town for one of Dad's annual work conferences, so I would have been all alone if it wasn't for him. I couldn't have asked for a better big brother. He stood by my side when I needed him to, and I leaned on him when it all became too much.

We were on our second Will Farrell movie when the doorbell rang. I nestled deeper into the couch and pulled the blanket up to my chin. I was a mess, and there was no way I was answering the door like this.

Aiden rolled his eyes and stood. "Don't worry. I'll get it," he offered sarcastically. Whoever was there grew impatient and started banging on the door. "All right, all right. I'm coming," Aiden warned the person on the other side. "Son of a bitch," he bit out, glancing through the peephole. He flung open the door and immediately took a step forward. "What the fuck are you doing here?"

I stiffened. Who was he talking to? Surely it wasn't-

"Is she here?" That was Dalton's voice. He sounded desperate.

"Is *who* here, *pal?*" Aiden said, his voice tinged with a sneer. There was a moment of silence before Dalton spoke again.

"I need to talk to Taylor. It's important."

"Anything you need to say to her, you can say to me. Or are we keeping secrets from each other now?" *Shit. This was about to get ugly.*

"It's not what you think."

"It's not what I think?" Aiden parroted, his volume increasing. "Are you fucking kidding me?" He was seething and I feared for Dalton's safety, but I didn't dare move. "I sent my sister on that trip with you, hoping you two could *finally* have a chance with each other-" *Wait, what?* "and what did you do? You fucked her for days and led her on, making her believe you guys had something special, just to come home and go running back into Gianna's cheating arms."

What was happening? Did my brother just admit to throwing us together on purpose? He knew this whole time? My head was spinning so fast, I almost missed Dalton's reply.

"That's not true. It's more complicated than that."

"I don't care how complicated it is! I just had to watch my baby sister fall completely apart because my best friend tore her heart out and stomped all over it."

His words made my chest ache all over again. I pulled the blanket up to my mouth to muffle my sobs. I didn't know how much more I could take.

"She's pregnant, Aiden." Dalton raised his voice, clearly over the need to defend himself. "Gianna is having my child. I can't just abandon her."

Aiden was quiet for a moment before speaking again. "How do you know it's yours?"

"What?" Dalton asked, sounding surprised. I hadn't thought of that either, but it was a valid question.

"Dude, she was fucking somebody else while you two were engaged."

"She's too far along. I saw the ultrasound picture. She's almost ten weeks. She didn't even know Antonio then!"

"You're an idiot." Aiden sighed and I chanced a glance over my shoulder. I could see him standing at the open door but couldn't see outside. I hoped Dalton didn't come into the house, because he would surely see me if he did. "She could be lying to you. She called off your wedding for this guy. You think she hasn't known him longer than two and a half months?"

Dalton didn't respond. He was either mulling over the possibility or getting ready to throw a punch at Aiden for basically calling the mother of his child a slut.

"Why would she lie about it if it could be his? She broke up with him because she's having *my* baby."

"Why would she lie to you?" Aiden repeated incredulously. "Because you're safe. You have a good job, money, a home. Are you so dense that you can't see that?"

"Gianna has her own money. She doesn't need mine," Aiden countered.

"She has her *parents'* money. There's a big difference."

"What does it matter? It's still not a good enough reason to lie."

"Mark my words, James. There's something fishy about this and you're going to end up getting fucked over."

"Look," he began, his voice heavy with exasperation, "I came here to talk to Taylor. Where is she?"

"She's not here."

"Bullshit. Her car is in the driveway."

"How do you know somebody didn't pick her up?" Aiden asked. It almost sounded like a taunt. "She could be out on a date right now. It's not like you two are seeing each other." Yep, definitely a taunt.

"Please, just let me talk to her," Dalton pleaded. "I have too much respect for you to enter your house against your will."

"But not too much respect to fuck with my sister and break her heart?"

There was a whoosh and suddenly the door slammed shut. I heard the lock click into place, followed by a loud crash. Aiden walked back into the room rubbing his knuckles.

"I'm so sorry," I said, tears dampening my cheeks again.

"What do you possibly have to be sorry for?"

"For coming between you two. You guys have been best friends for almost twenty years and I ruined it."

"No you didn't." He reached over and put his arm around my shoulders, giving them a squeeze. "Dalton is the one who screwed up. If he doesn't fix it, then the downfall of our friendship will be on his hands."

twenty

WHAT WAS I GOING to do? My best friend hated me, the woman I wanted to be with thought I was a lying, cheating piece of shit just like her ex, and I was going to be a father in roughly seven months, give or take. I had royally screwed up. My life took a nosedive in Seattle. I knew I should've just stayed on that island with Taylor. We'd be sipping Mai Tais on the beach right now, watching the tide come in. Instead, I was trying to figure out where I was going to put a crib and changing table.

Gianna and I needed to have a talk. Now that the shock had worn off, we needed to figure out where to go from here. I wasn't in love with her anymore and didn't want to lead her on. I wanted to be there for her and the baby, but she needed to know we'd never be a couple again.

She wanted to move in with me and pick up where we left off. I'd been fielding her advances since she ambushed me at my hotel. She was practically throwing herself at me, but I wouldn't do it. She thought I was just worried about the baby and tried to assure me it was perfectly safe to have sex while pregnant. I knew that. I just didn't want to. Not with her, at least. The only woman I wanted was sitting across town thinking I tossed her aside for a woman who'd already done me dirty once.

I cringed when Gianna walked into my house, tossing her keys onto the counter. They clinked loudly on the granite, followed by the grating sound of her voice calling my name.

"In here," I responded from the guest bedroom.

"There you are!" she cooed a few seconds later as she entered the room. She moved in for a kiss and I turned my head, her lips landing on my cheek. She played it off like that was what she'd been aiming for, but I saw the hurt flash in her eyes.

It made me feel like the world's biggest prick. She was trying to reconcile with me for the sake of our unborn child and I couldn't even bring myself to kiss her. Maybe I was being petty, punishing her for cheating, but she no longer held the allure she once did. Yeah, she was still technically sexy with her feminine curves, still-slender waist, and long, dark hair, but I knew what lay underneath and it wasn't all that pretty.

"Is this where we're putting the nursery?"

Not we, I wanted to tell her. *I*. This was where *I* was putting the nursery. This was where he or she would sleep while staying with me. "Yeah," I answered instead. That talk would come soon enough. No need to get her all upset right now.

"Mom and Dad want us to come over for dinner," she began, a hopeful gleam in her eye.

I'd agreed to a few meals and outings with her parents since they were going to be in my life forever now. Might as well get along with them. Besides, I'd always liked them. They were good to me. They'd spoiled Gianna and were mostly responsible for her being self-absorbed and financially dependent on others, but they were good people.

"Okay," I agreed easily. "What time do we need to be there?"

"Not until seven. That gives us plenty of time," she said suggestively, her eyes falling to my lips as she leaned her body into mine. I moved away from her, steadying her with my hands at her elbows so she wouldn't fall.

"I've got to get a little work done before we go. I'll pick you up at your place."

Her face fell and she took a step back. "Oh."

She looked dejected, but I couldn't let her reel me back in. If I went there again there would be no turning back. I'd never get another chance with Taylor, and that was what I was waiting for. I was biding my time until this whole mess got sorted out and I could beg her forgiveness. I just hoped it wasn't too late by the time I got my chance.

I sat through dinner with Jillian and Frank Venetti, Gianna's parents. He was a robust Italian man in his fifties with a thick, black mustache and hair generously peppered with grey. She was a waif of a woman with the same blue eyes as Gianna and strawberry blonde hair. Those baby blues were the only thing Gianna got from her mother. The rest of her was all Venetti.

"Have you guys thought about names yet?" Jillian asked, placing her napkin on the table next to her plate. We finished our desserts and were ready for coffee. I was glad I hadn't taken a drink of mine already, or I would have spit it out all over their nice table. I had barely come to terms with being a father. Baby names weren't even on the radar yet. "I know it's still early, but that's one of the most exciting things about having a baby," she gushed.

"Not yet," I offered with a tight smile. My fingers curled into my thighs as nerves overtook me. Gianna took that as her cue to offer me comfort. She wrapped her fingers around mine and I fought the urge to shake her off. I didn't need her touch, didn't want it. But I had to play nice. Not just for her parents, but for our child.

After dinner, I drove Gianna back to her condo. She hesitated before opening her door to get out. "Can you walk me up? I hate coming in at night."

I couldn't really say no, could I? Her safety was paramount, and if she felt she needed to be escorted to her door, I wouldn't hesitate.

"This neighborhood isn't what it used to be," she lamented as she punched the code to get into her building. I pushed the door open and waited until she stepped inside to follow. "It's not as safe as it was when I moved in." She only moved in about six months before we got engaged. The neighborhood hadn't changed *that* much. Maybe she was more cautious now that it wasn't just her she needed to worry about.

"If security is an issue, we can find you a new place."

Her shoulders sagged with disappointment and it took me a moment to realize why. She wanted me to offer to let her move into my house. That was the plan at one time. Her lease was up in a couple months, but she would've already moved in with me if we'd gotten married. Now she would need to sign a new lease or find somewhere else to live. If she needed help, I wouldn't hesitate to help her, but she wasn't moving in with me. There was no place for her there anymore.

We stopped outside her door and she pulled her keys from her purse. "Want to come in for a minute?"

She looked at me hopefully and my heart twisted inside my chest. It was about to tear me in two. Part of me wanted to say yes, to just give in. Like it or not, we were going to be a family. It would be so much easier if I just went with it, if we got back together and raised our child in a two-parent home, like the one I dreamed of as a boy. But how long would that be the easier option? She'd damaged our relationship beyond repair. I no longer looked at her like I once did. I didn't see the love of my life and the woman I wanted to grow old with anymore. Part of me would always love her, but I wasn't *in* love with her, and it wasn't fair to either of us to pretend.

I sighed and placed my hands on her shoulders. This was going to suck, but it had to be done. I couldn't beat around the bush anymore. She didn't do subtlety, so I would have to be blunt with her. I just hoped she didn't try to keep me from my child as punishment for what I was about to do.

Twenty-One

TWELVE MISSED CALLS. **MAYBE** I was crazy. Maybe I was obsessive, but I couldn't bring myself to clear out my call log because I liked seeing how many times Dalton had tried to get a hold of me. He called me three times that night, but only left one voicemail. I listened to it once, not allowing myself the chance to wallow in it before deleting it. It didn't matter. I knew it by heart.

Taylor, I need to talk to you. I need to explain. This isn't the end. It's just an intermission. Please, call me back.

Intermission, my ass.

He called three times the next day, and three the day after. The following day was two, then one, then none at all. He gave up and part of me felt relieved. The other part of me was disappointed all over again. I went back to work and fell into a normal routine. I half feared Gianna and Dalton would show back up, but they didn't. At least not together.

It had been nine days since the moment I learned they were back together— not that I was counting or anything— when Gianna came waltzing in with three of her friends. I was working the floor so I didn't have to seat them, but they were placed in the section adjacent to mine. They were just two tables away from my closest customers and I could feel the heat of Giana's glare on my back when I was taking down orders. I avoided her gaze at all cost, not daring to look toward her and her friends. When two of my tables emptied at once, I collected my tips and took a much-needed bathroom break.

I was reaching for the toilet paper when two female voices entered the restroom giggling. I froze, hoping one of those voices didn't belong to Gianna. Two sets of heels came into view beneath the stall door as they stood in front of the mirror. They were probably reapplying their lipstick after taking two miniscule bites of salad.

"Can you believe what she's doing to Dalton?" My ears perked up at the mention of his name. It was one of Gianna's friends.

"Why? What's she doing?" the other friend asked.

"She didn't tell you?"

"I know she's trying to convince him to let her move in because of the baby, but he's keeping her at arm's length to punish her," she harrumphed, clearly offended on Gianna's behalf.

"You are so naive, Jacklyn," the other woman scoffed.

What were they talking about? If Gianna was doing something behind Dalton's back, he had a right to know, didn't he? A thought occurred to me while they were gabbing. Unbeknownst to them, they were about to reveal something big and I had to ensure Gianna didn't get away with whatever scheme she'd concocted. I pulled out my phone and started a voice recording.

"You know the baby isn't his, right?" A loud gasp echoed throughout the room. I covered my mouth to conceal my own shocked reaction.

"You're kidding!" Jacklyn exclaimed. "How do they know already?"

"Simple DNA test."

"Does Dalton know?"

"Of course not. Do you think he'd be sticking around if he did?"

"So, who's the father? Is it Antonio?" There was no reply, but the first woman must've nodded her head because she was met with a "No way!" and a "Does he know?"

"Nope. She had them collect his blood then told him it wasn't a match."

"Why would she do that? I thought she loved Antonio."

"She does, but her parents threatened to cut her off if she stayed with him. They were furious when she broke off her engagement to Dalton."

"Do they know the baby isn't his?"

"God, no. They would be devastated."

"That is messed up," Jacklyn protested.

"So messed up," the other woman agreed.

They both entered stalls and I snuck out of mine, washing my hands quickly before I could get caught. My mind was reeling with what I'd just learned.

Gianna tricked Dalton into thinking he got her pregnant, when in reality it belonged to the man she was cheating on him with. She lied. About everything. She'd been sleeping with this Antonio guy longer than she'd admitted, which was why Dalton didn't think it was possible the baby belonged to Antonio based on how far along she was. I had to do something. Dalton had a right to know he was being tricked into remaining in Gianna's life.

He grew up without his father. The loser split because he couldn't handle the responsibility. Dalton never wanted to be like that, and Gianna knew it. She was using that to keep him close, and it was only a matter of time before she sank her claws into him so deep, he'd never be able to wriggle out of her grasp. If this went on and she managed to get away with this deception, he'd be stuck with her forever. Once that baby got here and Dalton took responsibility for it, he would never turn his back on it, whether his by blood or not.

And poor Antonio... He would miss out on everything because of Gianna's lies. She was keeping a man from his child for her own selfish benefit. She could get by with it though, which she knew. Both men had dark hair and dark eyes. Antonio's child could easily pass for Dalton's.

Even though I was devastated and furious with him for what he'd done, I had to do the right thing. I couldn't let him continue to believe a lie that would forever alter the path of his future.

twenty-two

ANOTHER **DINNER WITH THE** Venettis was in the books. I didn't know how many more times I could sit there and listen to her parents talk about how glad they were that I was back in the picture and how happy the news of Gianna's pregnancy made them. They apparently didn't care much for Antonio.

I had to endure Gianna hanging all over me at dinner and afterwards as we visited with her family. I couldn't peel her hands from my arm and back without them noticing, and she'd asked me not to break the news to them that we weren't back together after our long chat the other night.

"Please don't tell them," she begged, tears welling in her eyes. "They're so glad you're back in my life. It would break their hearts." Then she asked the one question I hadn't wanted to

answer. *"Do you think you'll ever be able to forgive me and give us another chance?"*

"Gianna..." I began, unsure how to break the news to her. I'd already made it clear that we weren't a couple, and that just because she was pregnant with my child, it didn't mean we were back together. I couldn't just forget that she'd slept with someone else and called off our wedding for him, ruining any chance at a future for us. But she was more emotional than usual, thanks to the pregnancy hormones, and I didn't want to be the cause of her next breakdown. *"Let's just try to get through the next six months without putting too much pressure on ourselves. We need to focus on the baby for now."*

That was my way of letting her down easy, but I wasn't sure she got it. She was still touching me more than necessary and leaning in to kiss my cheek every time we parted ways. She'd even been bold enough to go on about how much the surge of hormones had increased her sex drive. This whole subtle don't-upset-the-pregnant-lady approach wasn't working, and if she kept on like she was, I'd be forced to tell her it was never going to happen and possibly suffer her wrath.

She was exhausted when I dropped her off at her condo, so she didn't put up too much of a fight this time. When I arrived home, there was a familiar car parked in my driveway. I pulled up next to it and shut off the engine, hesitating a moment before getting out. Walking up to my front entrance, I noticed Aiden sitting on the steps leading up to my porch and my guard went up. The last time I saw him, I thought he was going to kick my ass. He wanted to. I could see it in his eyes. I hurt his sister and he wanted to make me pay. I hoped he'd cooled down since then.

"'Bout time you got home," he said in greeting, rising from the step.

"What are you doing here?" I was wary of his motive for being here, so I kept my distance. If he decided to throw a punch, I wanted to be out of his reach.

He let out a slow breath and a feeling of dread settled around me. "I've got something to tell you. Can we go inside?"

"Sure." I unlocked the door and led him inside. We walked to the kitchen and I flipped on the light, motioning for him to have a seat at the bar.

"You got any beer?"

"Yeah."

"Grab two. We're both going to need it."

What the hell? "Okayyyy." I drew out the word, letting it hang in the air. Reaching into the fridge, I grabbed two beers, handing his over before opening my own.

"Might want to take a seat."

I sat on the third stool at the bar, leaving an empty one between us. "What's this all about?"

"Taylor wanted me to bring something to your attention," he began, and I balked at the mention of her.

"Why couldn't she just tell me herself?" I was dying to see her so I could explain myself to her. At the time, I thought I was doing the right thing by putting things on hold with her while I figured out this whole pregnancy issue with Gianna, but once again I was wrong. I should have just waited and talked to her when I got back, but I panicked. I was a coward, too afraid to face her, which ended up hurting her more.

"I think you and I both know the answer to that." He was right. The look on her face when she saw me with Gianna nearly broke me. "She doesn't want to see you, especially after you came into her restaurant flaunting your pregnant ex-fiancé in her face, but-"

"Wait a minute." I held my hand up. "I wasn't flaunting anything, and I didn't know she worked there."

"How could you *not* know? She told you she got the job!"

"She only told me that she got a job as a hostess. I assumed she was working at Exeter."

"Well, shit."

"What?"

"She thought you took Gianna there on purpose, to drive the point home that the two of you were back together."

"We're *not* back together," I declared hotly, my voice harsher than I intended. One eyebrow ticked up in suspicion, but I continued. "We're having a baby and I'm trying to be supportive. I want to be there for her, for both of them."

"Yeah, about that..." His voice trailed off and he averted his gaze.

"What? Just spit it out already." I was growing impatient. He had a message from Taylor, and it sounded important.

Aiden took a deep breath. "Okay, okay. Gianna and her friends came into Francesca's for lunch today, and Taylor overheard a conversation between two of them in the bathroom," he began, curling his lip like the thought of Taylor in the bathroom disgusted him. "They were talking about Gianna lying to you."

My back straightened and I leaned forward. "Lying to me? About what?

"About the baby."

My hackles rose and I gritted my teeth. This serious. These accusations were serious. I needed to know the rest. "What about the baby?"

"Man, I'm sorry to be the one to tell you this," he began, genuine remorse flitting across his face, "but the baby isn't yours."

I shot up from my seat, knocking over the barstool in my haste. "What?" I shouted. "How could you possibly know that?"

"She had a DNA test. The baby belongs to Antonio, but she doesn't want anyone to know."

"Bullshit!" I snapped, even though I'd had my suspicions. I just didn't believe she could deceive me like that.

"Apparently her parents threatened to cut her off financially when she broke up with you and moved Antonio in. They didn't like him and didn't approve of the relationship." That much I knew was true. "When she found out about the baby and realized it was his, she hatched a plan to get you back so she could be back in her parents' good graces."

"I don't believe this." My anger boiled over and I kicked another barstool into the floor. I gripped my hair and pulled at it in frustration.

"I have the recording."

"The recording?"

"When Taylor realized they were talking about you, she started recording on her phone. She was afraid you wouldn't believe her without proof, and Gianna would get away with lying to you."

My chest constricted and I nearly cried. How could she think I wouldn't believe her? Did she really think there was no trust between us? Of course she did. *I* broke that trust when I didn't trust her enough to work through our newfound relationship after Gianna dropped this bombshell on me. On top of that, she thought I was rubbing Gianna in her face. No wonder she refused to see me or answer my calls. My mind was racing, so the rest of what Aiden said fell on deaf ears.

"What?" I asked when I saw him looking at me expectantly. He was holding his phone up, his finger hovering above the screen.

"I said, 'do you want to hear the recording?'" There was no way I'd ever want to hear it. It was bad enough getting it second-hand. "Taylor sent it to me, and-"

"Shit. Taylor!" I said in a panic. "I have to talk to her. I have to fix this." I headed for the door but didn't get very far. Aiden grabbed me and I spun on him, breaking his hold on my upper arm.

"I don't think so."

"Why the hell not?"

"I don't want you anywhere near her after everything you put her through. You had one chance with her and you blew it."

"I'm not ready to give up on her."

"I'm warning you, James, stay away from her." He'd warned me before and I obeyed, and it cost me years of happiness with a woman I loved with a desperation I'd never experienced before.

The woman I loved.

Until now, I hadn't realized that was what this feeling was. It wasn't just chemistry or attraction or companionship. I loved her. And I knew with every fiber of my being I would do anything to be with her, even if it meant going against my best friend. I respected his wishes back then and look where *that* got me.

"I'm sorry, Aiden, but I don't give a fuck about your warnings anymore. Nothing will keep me from being with her. That is, if she'll still have me."

"If you hurt her again, I'll break both your legs."

"Then I'll beg her forgiveness from my wheelchair." The corner of his lip quirked up and he nodded his head. "Lock up on your way out," I instructed, grabbing my keys and heading out the door. I needed to win her back. I'd worry about the rest in the morning.

twenty-three

Taylor

MY GLASS OF WINE was so full, I had to take a few little sips as I carried it from the kitchen to the family room so I wouldn't spill any. I had my remote, a chilled bottle of Riesling, and a stack of rom coms. I was ready for a cozy night at home. My parents were at a dinner party and Aiden appeared to be gone for the evening, so I had the place to myself. I was halfway through *Wedding Crashers* when there was a knock at the door. I hit pause and set my glass on the end table, ensuring it was on a coaster. My mom would freak if she came home and discovered I wasn't using one. God forbid I put a ring on her fancy end table that no one was allowed to actually use.

I made my way to the door, pulling my slouchy, open-front sweater closed and straightening my lounge pants. I'd been a slob since I came home this evening. My bra was the first thing to go, then my curled hair went into a bun. The stretchy pants and camisole were all I needed for my solo Vince Vaughn marathon. There was no one here to impress.

I glanced through the peephole and took a step back. Dalton was standing on my front porch. Why was he here? I looked again just to be sure I wasn't imagining things, and sure enough there he was, running his fingers through that glorious dark hair. He reached up and knocked again, startling me.

"Taylor, answer the door. I know you're in there. Your brother said you were home."

Aiden told him I was here? That meant he must have told Dalton about Gianna. Was he here to make up with me now that he knew about her lies? Screw that! I wouldn't be his second choice. I would never be someone's second choice or a dirty little secret ever again. If I couldn't be somebody's number one, I wouldn't be their anything.

I steeled myself against his charms and flipped the lock, opening the door to a distraught-looking Dalton.

"Thank God," he said, stepping up to me. I took a step back to keep a little distance between us. I couldn't think straight with him so close to me.

"What are you doing here?"

"I came to thank you," he began, "and to apologize." I stood there with my arms crossed over my chest, waiting for him to continue. "Can I come in?" he asked sheepishly, unsure of himself. He was usually so confident, it was satisfying to see him like this. I stepped aside and motioned for him to come in.

"Taylor, I-" he began, but stalled. "I have no words. There's so much I want to say, but I don't know where to begin." I remained silent. I wouldn't make this easier for him.

"I'm so sorry. I made a huge mistake in Seattle. Gianna flew out there and surprised me at my hotel."

"Ugh, I can't listen to this." Disgusted, I turned to walk away. He grabbed my arm, but I pulled out of his grasp. "Don't touch me," I warned, tears threatening to spring free at any moment.

"That's... I didn't mean it like that. I didn't... We didn't... Shit, I'm screwing this up."

"You can say that again," I huffed and rolled my eyes, crossing my arms obstinately.

"She'd been calling and texting and wouldn't leave me alone. She insisted we needed to talk, and when I told her I would probably be out of town for a couple weeks, she flew out there to tell me she was pregnant."

"What day was that?" Pain flashed in his eyes, which was all the answer I needed. He'd given me the cold shoulder after that, then called it quits on me.

Instead of answering, he added, "I never wanted us to be over. I just had to put it on hold for a while until I figured things out with Gianna."

"So, you wanted me to just sit around and pine after you while you played house with her?"

"No, I never wanted you to pine after me. I wanted to get to a point where I could be in my kid's life and have an amicable relationship with its mother. I didn't want you in the middle of it. I felt like it was something I needed to have a good handle on before we could even think about having a serious relationship."

"Are you sleeping with her?" I knew what her friends had said about him keeping her at arm's length, but I wasn't sure exactly what that meant. Was he holding her off emotionally, physically, or both?

"No," he declared adamantly. "We're not even together."

"Then why did you come to the place where I worked, knowing I would see you two together?"

"I didn't know that's where you were working. I thought you worked at Exeter." He stepped closer to me as he spoke, and this time I didn't back up. "I never would have brought her there if I'd known."

"Why did you think I worked at Exeter?"

"You never told me where you got a job. I just assumed, since you mentioned wanting to work there before, that's where you'd interviewed."

"But why were you there with *her* if you aren't together? It looked like a date."

He sighed sadly. "Her parents insisted on taking us to lunch. They wanted to celebrate." He winced, and I knew he was remembering my reaction to seeing them together. "I tried to talk to you. I wanted to explain." His eyes filled with melancholy as he took another step toward me. I read the sincerity in his face and I softened, my cool resolve melting away.

"Gianna and I were never together after me and you, and we never will be," he proclaimed.

He was standing so close to me now that I had to tilt my chin up to look at him. His eyes were haunted, like a man who'd been through hell and back over the last few weeks. Maybe he had. His clean, masculine scent invaded my nose and I longed to curl into him, to press my face into his neck like I had when we laid in bed after making love.

"I'm so sorry," he said, sliding his palm against my cheek. "About everything. I should have just told you. I should have let you decide what you were willing to stick around for, but I panicked. I had to make my child priority number one, because I know what it's like to not be a priority at all."

His declaration broke me, forcing a sob from my lips. I hated that Gianna had done this to him, to *us*. She wedged herself between us before we even had a chance to solidify what we had, what we were feeling. And it was all because she didn't want to lose her monthly stipend.

"Can you forgive me?" he asked, his hand sliding to the back of my neck and his eyes dropping to my lips.

I could. I wanted to. I just had to allow myself to give in. Was I willing to trust him with my heart again? It was a toss-up. He had the power to destroy me completely, but this could be my one chance at happiness, too. If I said no, I'd always regret not finding out what we could've been.

"Yes," I breathed, and his lips crashed down on mine. I opened to him— my mouth, my arms, my heart. He angled my head perfectly for his invading mouth. His other arm snaked around my waist and crushed me to him. My heart soared. This was what I'd been missing since we got back. I forgot how good it felt to be held by him, to have his warm, strong arms wrapped around my body.

He deepened the kiss and I moaned. Both hands were now on my waist and sliding beneath my sweater. His kiss stole my breath, and my nipples puckered behind the thin fabric of my camisole as his chest brushed against mine.

"Taylor, I need you," he declared, his voice thick with emotion. He was shaken and vulnerable, but he didn't try to hide it. He let me see him. He let me see every part, every flaw. And I drank him in, wanting to know it all.

His hard body was plastered to mine and I could feel the extent of his desire pressing against my stomach.

"Dalton," I sighed, my head lolling to the side when his lips moved to my neck. It felt good to give in. I'd been hell-bent on staying mad at him, at refusing him if he came back around, but my heart wasn't in it. My heart wanted him. It always had.

"Take me upstairs," I whispered. Our need was growing beyond our ability to contain it. We would combust if we didn't do something about it. He didn't hesitate. I was in his arms with my thighs clamped around his torso in seconds. He found the stairs and ascended them as quickly as he could while carrying me in his arms.

"Is your room the same?" He probably hadn't been up here in years. I'd be surprised if he remembered any of the rooms.

"Yeah, it's right-" He was turning the knob before I could finish. I guessed he *did* know which one was mine. It was the same one it had been for the last fifteen years.

"I know exactly where it is," he growled against my mouth. "I used to walk by as slowly as I could, hoping you would come out at just the right moment and I'd catch a glimpse of you."

His confession shocked me. I never realized he was standing on the other side of that door hoping to see me as much as I hoped to see him. If I heard Aiden and his friends coming up the stairs, I'd wait until they got to the top and then walk to the bathroom, or pretend I needed something from the kitchen. I was disappointed when it was one of Aiden's other friends, but when it was Dalton, my heart would race. I'd wear my cutest outfit and fix my hair if I knew he was coming over. Most of the time I didn't have any warning and ended up looking like a troll when he was around.

Dalton carried me to my bed and laid me down gently, covering my body with his. He kissed me like he'd gone years without kissing anybody at all. He was starved for my touch and I was happy to satiate him.

"I've missed you so much." He feathered kisses over my face and along my jaw, returning once again to my lips. "I was miserable without you. I'm so sorry for putting you through all this," he apologized again.

"I know," I assured him, cupping his face with my hands. His stubble scraped against my palm and I welcomed the friction. I loved his face when it went untouched by a razor. "And it's okay. We'll figure this out."

His lips returned to mine and he kissed me like he did that first time on the beach. It was desperate and needy and full of relief. My lips parted and his tongue dove inside. I met his invasion with my own, our mouths becoming one. He flexed his hips, grinding his erection against my center.

"Condom," I demanded, needing him inside me right this minute. I couldn't go any longer without having him. He pulled away from me and pressed his forehead against mine.

"Damn it," he mumbled breathlessly. "I didn't bring any." My face fell as disappointment surged in my veins.

"I don't think I have one, either." He lifted his face and studied me for several seconds. His eyes widened at the exact moment a solution came to my mind.

"Aiden," we said in unison. He lifted off me and we scrambled from the bed. I opened the door and tiptoed across the hall to Aiden's room. Dalton went to the stairs to keep watch just in case my big brother decided to choose this very inopportune moment to return home. I snuck inside and went to his bedside table. I was sure he'd have some in there.

He won't notice any are missing if I just take one, right?

I rifled through the drawer until I spotted a familiar black box. I tore one foil packet off the roll and went to shut the drawer, but hesitated. *Maybe I should take two, just in case.* I grabbed another one before shoving the rest inside the box and putting everything else back where I found it. His door clicked shut behind me and Dalton turned to face me. His eyes darkened, the chocolate brown turning almost black as he took me in. They raked over my body as he stalked toward me. My breathing accelerated and my pulse spiked, my steady heartbeat turning into a gallop.

Dalton plucked the condoms from my hand and backed me into my room, kicking the door shut once inside. He placed them on my nightstand and brought his hands to my shoulders, his thumbs feathering over my collarbones before hooking beneath the edges of my sweater. He slowly pushed the fabric down my arms, the soft material sliding over my skin. It was extra sensitive, and I was hyper aware of every single sensation. Goosebumps spread across my arms, but it wasn't from being cold. I was on fire for him. Anticipation and excitement caused my skin and nipples to pebble.

Once my sweater was gone, his hands found the edge of my shirt, his fingers dipping under the hem to graze my stomach. He lifted it, his fingers leaving a trail of molten lust in their wake as they skimmed over my ribs and breasts. I raised my arms above my head so he could slip my top off completely. His hands immediately went to the waistband of my pants. He plucked at the drawstring, releasing the little bow I had tied there. He drew out the motion, and I grew more and more impatient with every second that passed.

I sucked in a breath when he knelt in front of me and tugged at the loose fabric at my hips. My pants slid down my legs and he leaned forward, pressing his lips to my lower belly. I stepped out of them when they pooled at my feet. Dalton stood and removed his shirt. We didn't speak a word as I reached for the button on his pants and popped it free. I unzipped him; my movements, fueled by lust and impatience, were much faster than his had been.

He let out a muted chuckle as I pushed his pants down his legs.

Once they were off, he lifted me and placed me in the center of my bed. Kissing me sweetly, he moved his lips lower, trailing scorching hot kisses down my body until he reached the edge of my panties. They were plain white cotton, not the sexy satin and lace I'd worn on our trip, but he didn't seem to notice or care. He just wanted them off and I concurred.

I held my breath as he hooked his fingers beneath the edges and shimmied them down my legs. I was finally bare to him and I couldn't wait to have his hands and mouth on me, not to mention the steel length currently tenting his boxers several inches away from his body. I swallowed hard, remembering how he felt, how full I'd been when he buried himself inside me. Was my body still accustomed to his size after weeks of being apart? I supposed we were about to find out.

He settled between my legs and kissed my lower belly again, moving down my pelvis. My legs fell open for him on instinct, as though I had no control over them. His hot tongue darted out, finding my clit, and my back arched off the bed. That one quick swipe sent a shockwave of pleasure through my core. His large hands framed my hips, pinning me into place. His tongue swirled and I writhed as he brought me to the edge. A high cry of pleasure escaped my lips as my orgasm crashed over me.

"Fuck, I missed that sound," he declared, crawling back up my body. He kissed me long and deep as he rolled his hips and I bucked against him. My body was primed and sensitive, every nerve ending alight with hunger.

I needed him. Every touch, every sound he made, every word he spoke to me had my desire skyrocketing. I lifted my legs, digging my heels into his ass cheeks. They caught his boxers and I pushed against the fabric. My hands slid down the front of his body and grappled for the waistband. He realized what I was trying to do and lifted from my body to help me remove his underwear. I watched as he rolled the condom on and my need for him crescendoed.

I pushed myself off the bed and sat up on my knees. He met me in the middle, wrapping his arms around my waist as his lips found mine. I let him kiss me, his large hand gripping me by the nape as he slid his hot tongue over mine. I only granted him access for a few seconds before I pushed against his chest. When we broke apart, his eyes searched mine, looking to see what was wrong. He wouldn't find anything but passion and a poignant longing over a decade in the making.

I pressed forward until he had no choice but to sit and straddled his hips. He reached back with one arm to brace his weight and curled the other around my back, bringing our bodies flush with each other.

"Let your hair down," he requested, his voice husky and eyes hooded.

I did as he instructed and pulled the elastic band from my hair, letting the heavy strands fall over my shoulders. He speared his hands into it and brought my mouth to his. I lifted up just enough so he was poised at my entrance. He groaned against my lips and I felt the sound from the tips of my breasts to the tight channel between my legs that already pulsated with need. I lowered myself onto him slowly, letting my body stretch and adjust inch by pleasurable inch. We moaned in unison when he was fully seated inside me. I opened my eyes and found him watching me, a look of pure adoration brightening his dark brown irises. The sight made my heart flutter and my belly tighten. His look turned my insides to mush.

Needing to move, I flexed my hips and Dalton sucked in a sharp breath. His hands went to my hips, his fingers digging in as he gripped me tight. I leaned back, angling my body so he could hit all the right spots. His fingers found the tender bud just above where our bodies connected and circled it. Tension coiled tight in my lower belly as heat pooled between my thighs. After weeks without Dalton's touch, my orgasm was like a spring that had been compressed for too long. Once it was let go, it exploded violently, shaking my entire body.

Dalton flipped me onto my back and pounded into me. My orgasm was starting to wane when another took its place. My muscles clenched, gripping him tightly and pulling the climax from him as my body delivered another delicious release. He collapsed on top of me, breathing hard and barely holding his full weight off my body with his arms.

When he slipped out of me, I felt the loss more deeply than I could have imagined. That searing, soul-deep connection was broken and I wanted it back. He got up and walked to the door, giving me an unobstructed view of his perfectly sculpted backside. Everything from his back, to his ass, to his powerful hamstrings looked as though he'd been carved from marble. He was rock solid, his muscles perfectly cut and defined. He cracked the door open and peeked out into the hallway. When he saw the coast was clear, he stepped out, returning a minute later, the used condom discarded.

He pulled me into his arms, placing a soft kiss on my lips and then my forehead. "How the hell did I survive so long without that?" he asked, cradling me to his chest.

"The question is, how did *I*?" His chest vibrated with laughter.

"I'm glad we're on the same page."

Dalton turned down the covers and we slipped between the sheets. He brought our naked bodies together, pulling me into his embrace. My cheek rested against his chest and my arm was slung over his abdomen. His fingers stroked lightly over my back and arm, causing goosebumps to spread over my skin once again. After a few minutes his movements ceased and his whole body tensed.

"Where are your parents?"

"At a dinner party."

He released a breath and continued running his fingers over my skin. "I hope they haven't come home in the last twenty minutes."

"Psh, try ten," I taunted with a giggle.

"What?" he said, sitting up and feigning offense. "It was at least fifteen."

"Twelve, tops," I teased. He rolled us over, landing on top of me.

"Fourteen," he countered, pinning my arms above my head.

"Twelve and a half." The laugh fell from my lips at the heated look in his gaze.

"Thirteen." His eyes flashed to my mouth and my tongue darted out to lick my lips.

"Okay," I agreed huskily. "I'll give you that."

"What else will you give me?" He punctuated the question with a roll of his hips. He was hot and hard, his body ready for round two.

I reached down and palmed him in answer. He groaned and his lips descended to mine.

"Think you can make it to twenty minutes this time?"

"Think you can handle me for twenty minutes?"

I wasn't sure, but I was definitely up for the challenge.

And I was glad I grabbed that second condom.

twenty-four

I **WOKE TO WARM, VANILLA** scented skin and curled around the soft body lying next to me in the bed. *Taylor.*

Last night was intense. Weeks of misunderstandings, hurt feelings, and sexual frustration culminated in the best make up sex anyone has ever had. I'd come over here hoping she would let me explain what happened and hopefully forgive me for being such a damn idiot. I didn't expect explosive, mind blowing sex to follow.

She groaned and stretched before rolling over to face me. "Good morning."

Her smile was genuine and beautiful. I missed this. Having her wake up next to me, illuminated by the sunlight streaming in through the windows highlighting her freckles was something I'd yearned for and regretted losing.

"Good morning," I replied and pressed a quick kiss to her lips. "There are three people in this house who would be pissed if they knew I stayed over." Aiden and her parents couldn't know that I slept here last night. I didn't mean to fall asleep, but it felt so good having her back in my arms again and I was so tired. I was exhausted from trying to fight both my feelings for her, and Gianna's persistent advances.

Gianna.

I would have to face her. A confrontation was inevitable. And it needed to happen today.

I grabbed my phone and checked the time. It was almost eight, and I knew Mrs. Wesley would be up soon to start the coffee and then breakfast. "I better sneak out before everyone else in the house gets up."

"That's probably for the best."

Even though Aiden gave me the go ahead to come here and try to win his sister back, I was positive he wouldn't appreciate me spending the night in her bed. I reluctantly got out of bed and put the same clothes on that I'd worn last night. She rolled over onto her stomach, propping herself onto her elbows to watch me dress. I was half tempted to rejoin her, but I needed to get out of there.

I kissed her one last time and crept silently to the door and out into the hall. The stairs were just within reach when I heard a door creak open. Assuming it was Taylor wanting another kiss goodbye, I turned, a smile breaking out over my lips. It fell when I saw who was standing just outside his doorway.

"I see you two made up," Aiden deadpanned.

Shit. Why was he up so early on a Sunday?

"Yeah," was all I could offer. I hung my head. This might be worse than being caught by her father. Aiden knew everything. He knew the details of what went down between Taylor and me and I didn't know if he'd ever forgive me for it.

"I was serious about what I said last night. Don't hurt her again."

"I won't. She's it for me."

His body visibly relaxed. "It's about fucking time," he declared. "I've been watching you two dance around each other for years."

What the hell?

"You're the one who forbid me from dating her."

"Yeah, when we were like, seventeen."

I was incredulous. "Dude, all this time, I thought she was off limits. You never said the ban was lifted!"

"She's a fucking adult, numb-nuts. I have no say over who she dates. I just didn't want your horny teenage ass getting a hold of her back then. I would've been an uncle before I even went off to college if I hadn't warned you off her."

"Shit." I ran my fingers through my hair, frustrated that I'd spent all this time thinking it would jeopardize our friendship if I pursued his sister.

"I guess I could've told you all this sooner," he conceded. "I just assumed you were over her when you popped the question to Gianna. It never occurred to me that you two were still so hung up on each other."

"So you always knew and said nothing?" He just shrugged. I'd never wanted to punch my best friend in the face more than I did in that moment. "Asshole."

"I'm sorry, man. If I'd known she'd end up dating a whole string of losers, I would've pushed you two together a long time ago. As far as any man possibly being good enough for her, you come the closest."

"You mean I'm the only one, right?"

"Nah, man. Not even *you* are good enough for her. No one is."

I guessed I could understand that. I didn't have any siblings—at least none that I knew of— but I imagined I'd be just as protective over them if I did.

We said our goodbyes and I left there with the peace of mind that our friendship would survive this. It would take a little while to get back to normal, but it would happen eventually. The best part was that I no longer had to hide my attraction to Taylor. We were free to pursue a relationship without interference or sneaking around behind her brother's back.

The final obstacle was situated in a luxury condo across town, plotting to keep an unborn child from its father for her own benefit. I should give her a chance to come clean. Sit her down and ask for the truth. It would be hard to remain civil in light of her deception. What she was doing went far beyond anything a decent, reasonable human being would do. It made me wonder, not for the first time, how I could've loved her the way I had. She still had a lot of growing up to do, but immaturity was no excuse for the hell she'd put me through over the last couple months. And it certainly wasn't enough of a reason to deceive not one, but two men regarding the paternity of a child. She went too far this time, and there was no forgiving this indiscretion.

I sent her a quick text before pulling onto the street to head home, asking her to come over around noon. It was best to get this over with as soon as possible. I considered having her meet somewhere in public like she'd done when she ended our engagement, but I feared that would backfire on me. Instead of keeping her composure because there were people around like I had, I worried she'd do the opposite. This was going to be ugly, so we would have to do this in private.

She answered me back immediately, saying she would be there. I asked Aiden to send me the recording in case she tried to deny everything. The file came through just as I pulled into my driveway.

Even though I wanted to keep Taylor's scent with me all day, I needed a shower. I closed my eyes as the warm spray pelted my back and shoulders. Memories of my time spent with Taylor came flooding back. Her in the shower with me, us on the beach pretending we didn't want to rip each other's clothes off, that first night in the tub when I thought I'd combust if I didn't make love to her. She was everything I'd never let myself dream of before. I shut the water off and toweled myself dry before I let those thoughts go any farther.

As I poured a cup of coffee, I contemplated my approach with Gianna. If I came at her with guns blazing, she would freak out and shut down. She needed to stay calm and accept that I would no longer be a part of her life. I considered calling her parents so they could intervene if she got too out of control, but I wanted to give her a chance to do the right thing and come clean to them as well.

My front door opened at eleven thirty and I cringed. I would have to get that house key back from her somehow, or else get my locks changed. This was going to suck.

"Hey, D. I brought lunch," she called from the foyer. I met her in the kitchen as she sat the bag of takeout on the counter. I winced, realizing she thought this was some kind of date or happy get together. She would be sorely disappointed once she gleaned the true purpose of our meeting. She reached out to embrace me and plant her signature I'm-pretending-to-just-be-friendly kiss on my cheek. I grabbed her upper arms and held her at bay.

"We need to talk." Her smile fell and for the first time in weeks, she looked nervous. Even when we'd had our talk earlier and I told her we weren't going to be a couple again, she remained confident, but now she could sense something major was about to go down and her bravado slipped. I guided her to the living room and instructed her to sit on the couch while I took the chair adjacent to her.

"Gianna," I began, but had no fucking clue what to say. I'd gone over a hundred conversations in my head but still hadn't settled on one by the time she arrived, thirty minutes early. "I need you to be honest with me." *Let's lead with that, set the expectation.*

"Of course," she promised, but her hands were wringing in her lap, a dead giveaway that I'd already thrown her off-kilter. She clenched them together and settled them over her knee when she noticed me watching.

"The baby." I held her gaze. I wanted her to look me in the eye. I wanted her to tell the truth and confess on her own. "Who's the father?"

Her eyes darted to the side quickly and then settled back to me. "I don't understand."

"Tell me the truth." My calm demeanor and even tone belied the turmoil boiling just below the surface. "Who is the baby's father?"

She opened her mouth to speak but snapped it shut again. She wanted to lie, to keep the ruse going for her own selfish benefit, but she needed to fess up. Once she let her mask fall, it was obvious the guilt was eating at her. She'd been pretending for weeks. Pretending to still be in love with me, pretending that she'd all but forgotten Antonio, pretending to be carrying my child instead of his. Her lips trembled as tears pooled in her eyes.

"Dalton," she pleaded.

Gianna didn't want me to make her confess, but I needed to hear it from her. I wanted to be sure. Regardless of what she told me in the next few moments, I was going to be with Taylor. If, by some chance, the child turned out to be mine, I would honor my responsibility and shower my child with the love and affection my father never showed me. I would be there for Gianna, just not as a lover. But my gut was telling me that wasn't the case.

"Tell me." My command was gentle but left no room for argument.

"This wasn't supposed to happen!" she said, breaking into sobs.

"You lied to me."

"I never meant to hurt you."

"You tried to trick me into taking responsibility for another man's child!"

She cried harder. "I was losing everything. I had no choice!" Her voice rose in desperation.

"Of course you had a choice," I snapped, climbing to my feet quickly. My chest heaved with barely contained anger. "You could have grown the hell up and taken responsibility for yourself, for once in your life. You have a degree and countless connections. You could easily get a job and support yourself. You had a boyfriend that you obviously loved. I mean," I huffed out a humorless laugh, raking my hands through my hair, "you called off our wedding for him, so he must be very important to you. He should be the one helping to support you."

She scoffed, crossing her arms over her chest defiantly. "Antonio doesn't have a *real* job. He can't even sell enough of his paintings to put food on the table."

So she *was* his sugar mama.

"That's not an excuse. What you did was unforgivable. Hell, everything you've done the last couple months has been unforgivable. Did you ever really love me at all?"

"Yes," she answered on a strangled cry. "I still do. I'm just not *in* love with you anymore. And I think you feel the same way."

"You were sleeping with someone else *while we were engaged,* and canceled our wedding because of him. *Then* you lied to me about being pregnant with my child. Can you blame me for no longer being in love with you?"

"It happened before that."

"What?" I asked, taken aback. *How can she say that?*

"Things changed between us over the last year. The closer we got to the wedding, the more apparent it became that we weren't meant for each other."

"Like I said that night, you could've told me sooner."

"I kept thinking it was just pre-wedding jitters. For both of us. It wasn't until I met Antonio that I realized what was missing in our relationship."

That stung. Even though I never wanted her back and was ready to give my heart to Taylor, it hurt to hear those words come out of her mouth. But I needed to hear them.

"You have to tell everyone else the truth. Do your parents know?"

"No," she replied. Her shoulders sagged and her head hung shamefully. "They're going to lose it."

"Do you want them to come over here? Get it over with now?" Her eyes flashed to mine and widened in fear. I mentally kicked myself. Why did I offer to do that?

"I think I'd better tell Antonio first. He deserves to hear the truth before anyone else."

"You're right," I agreed. "He does."

"I'm so sorry for everything I've done to you." Tears leaked from the corners of her eyes again. "I panicked. I didn't know how I would live without my parents' support. It was the only solution I could think of at the time. You were out of the country, my parents weren't speaking to me, Antonio was spending hours in his studio, and I was throwing up every morning."

Somehow, she managed to make me feel sympathy for her. I had no doubt she was scared, and people often made irrational and sometimes devastating decisions out of fear. For that, I couldn't find it in me to hate her. I didn't love her, and I certainly didn't like her at the moment, but I didn't hate her.

"I'm not going to tell you it's okay because it's not, but I accept your apology." Forgiveness would come later. Her betrayal was just too fresh right now and I needed some distance.

She returned my house key without any fuss and I sent her on her way with the lunch she'd brought, encouraging her to meet up with Antonio. As mad as I was with her, he would be even more furious. At least, he should be.

I couldn't believe how smoothly that went. I expected her to deny everything, forcing me to produce the recording. She didn't even ask me how I knew. At least I didn't have to rat out her friend. If I had, that girl would rue the day she crossed Gianna Venetti.

With that mess cleaned up, I plopped down on my couch and kicked up my feet, switching on the TV. I hadn't been able to truly relax in weeks, and it was time to catch up with Sports Center.

At eight o'clock that evening, my phone rang and a photo I'd snapped of me and Taylor during that sunset cruise flashed across my screen. As promised, she was calling as soon as her shift was over. I hadn't told her about the meeting with Gianna yet. That wasn't a conversation I intended to have over text.

"Hey," I greeted.

"Hey yourself," she replied.

"How was work?"

"Good," she answered a little breathlessly. "Busy. I just got out."

"Are you tired?"

"Not really. I slept really well last night." She giggled as an answering grin formed over my lips.

"Wanna come over and watch a movie with me?"

"Sure. I can be there in twenty."

Here goes nothing.

"I was thinking maybe you could run home and pack an overnight bag before heading this way."

She was silent for a beat and I almost took it back. I knew we'd spent several nights together already, but this was different. Aside from Gianna, I'd never allowed another woman into my space. It was a big step inviting her to stay. She had me sweating bullets, waiting for her answer.

"I think I could manage that," she said finally, the smile audible in her voice.

Less than an hour later, she was snuggled against my side with my arm wrapped around her shoulders.

"What do you want to watch?" I asked, scrolling through our options.

"Anything with Tom Hardy."

"Tom Hardy, huh? Is that who does it for you?" I teased.

She bit her lip and shook her head, her eyes dancing with mischief.

"No? And who would that honor belong to?"

She turned, bracing one knee next to my hip and swinging her other leg over my lap. Her hands came up to my face and she looked into my eyes. My hands settled on her hips as I awaited her answer, suspecting I already knew what it would be.

"You," she said, the instant before her lips descended on mine. Her kiss started slow and sweet, but when I opened my mouth to deepen it, the heat behind it rose considerably. My hands slid beneath her shirt and skimmed up her back, luxuriating in the feel of her silky skin. She was soft and warm and smelled so damn good.

She rolled her hips and I groaned. The friction was enough to spark my desire without granting me any relief. I needed to get her shorts off and feel that hot, wet center against my skin. I stood, cradling her against me, her weight resting in my hands cupped beneath her ass.

I carried her down the hall and into my room, not releasing her until we were at my bed. She ran her hands over my shoulders and arms, exploring each muscle, her soft fingertips gliding almost reverently over my skin. I laid her across my bed and stood to remove my shirt. Her hazel eyes were rimmed with a ring of gold that seemed to blaze like an inferno.

I ran my hands up the outside of each thigh, watching her face and memorizing her reactions. I loved seeing how my touch affected her. When my fingers found the edge of her shorts, her lips parted on a silent gasp and her eyes widened ever so slightly. She lifted her ass, allowing me to remove her shorts. I wanted to go slow. I wanted to tease her, to draw out her satisfaction, but I couldn't wait any longer. I ripped her shorts down her legs and went back for her little pink thong. She pulled her shirt off hastily, her impatience matching my own.

We collided, skin on skin, our tongues diving inside each other's mouths for a taste. We were both needy and frantic, every motion fueled by lust and something a little deeper. I was falling. She was, too, if I was reading the situation right. We were two ships lost at sea, battered and bruised by the ones we'd loved before. We met in a raging storm and were finally sailing into calmer waters.

My chest filled with hope, my heart fluttering with excitement. Maybe it was too soon to get involved with someone else, but one thing was for certain. No one – not even Gianna – ever made me feel the way Taylor did. It took me those six days and nights to realize just what I'd been missing.

Epilogue

Taylor

Two years later...

I COULDN'T WAIT TO get back to this place. This was where it all began. The moment we stepped foot on this island sealed our fate. There was no escaping our attraction, the explosive chemistry that kept our bodies on high alert whenever the other one was near. We fought it for years, but those last few days when we tried to deny what we felt were the hardest. When we finally gave in, I swear, we heard the angels sing. It was that euphoric.

Our villa was wonderful, but nothing compared to the overwater bungalow Dalton secured for us this time. It was downright magical. We could step out of our bedroom and into the water in only a handful of steps. A few stairs were all that separated us from the clear blue

Caribbean Sea. There was a huge section of floor in our bedroom made of glass so we could see down into the ocean without ever going outside. The tub on our deck was more luxurious than the one we had before, and there was an infinity pool. He'd gone all out this time.

A little part of me felt pleased that he'd booked us a nicer place than he had for himself and Gianna when it was supposed to be their honeymoon. Rarely did I think of his ex-fiancé these days, and no longer felt insecure about not measuring up to her, but it was still satisfying to know he did more to impress me. Especially since I was far more easily impressed than she'd ever been.

Dalton often remarked on how low maintenance I was when we first started officially dating. It always surprised him when I opted for a low-key evening at home with him, a bottle of cheap wine, and a movie opposed to a fancy dinner and cocktails at the ritzy clubs downtown. He was shocked when I wanted to hit up Target for a new pair of jeans instead of Saks, and loved it when I went to the home improvement store with him in yoga pants and no makeup.

He was content. More than that, he was happy. He was the most relaxed I'd seen him in more than five years. It was a wonderful feeling, knowing I had something to do with that. Our love was effortless. That wasn't to say we didn't have disagreements on occasion, but it was rarely ever about anything major. Still, we always jumped at the opportunity for hot, semi-angry make up sex. That night in my room at my parents' house was just the beginning. When I moved in with him four months later, I'd pick a fight with him over leaving the toilet seat up just to stoke that fire.

It only took him a few weeks to catch on before he started doing it to me. Makeup left out on the bathroom counter? He'd find me sitting on the couch with my schoolbooks spread out over my lap and start pestering me about it. I'd get annoyed and try to push him away, and he'd have me on my back with my arms pinned above my head in seconds, punishing me with his thrusts. He'd make me wait to orgasm, drawing out the pleasure until I was ready to cry. I couldn't wait to pick a fight with him *here*. The aftermath would be so very satisfying.

The only serious fight we ever had was the day he confessed his role in getting the school off my back over the affair with my professor. He'd confided in his and my brother's friend Travis about what happened with Jason, and later, the meeting I'd had with the dean and his crony. Dalton and Travis decided to pay them a visit, setting up a meeting with the two of them under false pretenses. Travis was waiting on his results from the bar exam at the time, but he walked in there with the bravado of a seasoned attorney. Together they enlightened the scoundrels on how monumentally the two had screwed up and threatened legal action if they interfered in any way with the completion of my education. My account was unfrozen, and I had full access to register for classes shortly after, something I'd wondered about but was too excited to question at the time.

I was furious that he'd meddled in my business with the college. Even worse, he involved Travis, thus revealing my dirty little secret to yet another of my brother's friends. We didn't talk for two whole days while I seethed at my parents' house. When I finally gave in and answered his call, he explained why he did it. He was afraid they'd continue to sweep tenured professors' indiscretions under the rug and bully students into keeping quiet. Dalton dug into Dean Crawford's past and discovered he was Jason's mentor when he first began teaching at the university. He apparently instructed him on more than just how to teach at the college level. There were rumors of him engaging in affairs with students back in those days, but there was never any proof and no one willing to come forward. Jason carried on his legacy as Crawford worked his way up to dean. How he managed to secure that position, I'd never know.

Dalton said they were shaking in their boots by the time he and Travis left, promising I would be free to register for classes ASAP. He also assured me that he only told Travis the bare minimum about my indiscretions to secure his help and advice. Travis wasn't stupid, though. It wouldn't have taken him long to figure out the rest. Still, once I calmed down and was able to fully understand Dalton's motivation for interfering, I was able to see that he had saved me from a year of looking over my shoulder, waiting for the other shoe to drop. I wasn't being blackmailed into keeping quiet about a sleazeball professor manipulating young female students into affairs with him anymore, and that was incredibly freeing. He did it because he loved me and knew I'd be a basket case the entire year if I had that extra weight on my shoulders.

Thankfully, I never heard from Jason or the dean again. I found out through a classmate who'd taken some of Jason's classes along with me that Melody left him shortly after the baby was born. Good for her, for both of them.

Our first few days back on the island went much like the last few days of our previous trip to the resort. We sunbathed and made out in the water. His hands would find my ass and he'd grind his erection into my pelvis, then we'd end up in bed in the middle of the day, a mess of tangled limbs and salty skin. At night, we had dinner and walked on the beach, enjoying the entertainment and nightly parties. We put that infinity pool and tub on the deck to good use. I hoped our bungalow neighbors didn't see or hear any of our late-night activities, but in the end, I really didn't care.

On day four, I broke out that infamous red bikini he lost his mind over last time just to taunt him. He got all growly and possessive, just like I hoped. We had a good bit of privacy out there, but that didn't matter. That bikini incited his lust and inflamed his jealousy. I enjoyed the three minutes I got to wear it, but I enjoyed him taking it off me even more.

That evening we had early reservations for dinner, so we left our little private slice of paradise while the sun was still high in the sky. We feasted on crab legs and split lobster tail, washing it all down with generous amounts of sangria. The sun was sinking lower in the sky, casting the clouds in a riotous glow of orange and purple as we left the restaurant. We walked along the beach at a leisurely pace, passing a familiar little bar nestled right up to the sand. It was the place where Dalton had pulled me away from Nico to claim me as his own. I giggled at the memory, so glad he finally gave in and confessed his feelings for me.

"What's so funny?" Dalton asked, tugging on my hand. He pulled me closer and wrapped his arm around me as we walked.

"Do you remember that place?" I pointed up the beach.

"How could I forget?" His jaw ticked with annoyance and my pulse raced.

Maybe I should poke the bear some more. It could make our evening a little more fun.

"I was so mad at you for swooping in and ruining my night." His mouth flattened into a hard line and I chuckled. "Don't get your panties in a wad. I was glad afterward when I found out why you came in there all broody."

"I was *not* broody," he claimed defensively, but the corner of his mouth quirked up.

"You were *totally* broody. I thought you were going to challenge Nico to a duel." He threw his head back and laughed, the sound deep and rich, sending a vibration through my chest that settled in my stomach. I never knew a laugh could be so sexy.

"Hey, if you hadn't run off that evening and made me chase you down, I wouldn't have felt the need to get all broody. I was pissed," he admitted.

"I could tell." We both chuckled. Looking back, it was kind of funny. I'd screwed with him on purpose just to piss him off. It had the unexpectedly fabulous side effect of him going all caveman and carrying me back to our villa and making love to me. And for that, I wasn't the least bit sorry.

He slowed to a stop and I turned to look at him. He pulled me in close and placed a soft kiss on my lips. I wrapped my arms around his neck and lifted my gaze to his. His eyes were a warm chocolate brown at any other time, but tonight had taken on a more whiskey hue as the golden glow of the sunset reflected in them.

"Do you remember this spot right here? Where we're standing now?"

I glanced around, trying to recall the significance, but that night was a whirlwind, the landscape passing by in a blur.

"This is the spot where everything changed," he said when I didn't answer right away. "It's where we had our last first kiss."

"Our last first kiss?" I asked, perplexed. That didn't make any sense.

"Technically our first kiss was ten years ago, but we went so long before our next, it was like having our first kiss all over again." His sweet declaration brought a smile to my face. That first kiss in his old smelly Tahoe was a disaster. It started out perfect, but then he pushed me away, shattering my heart into a million pieces. The next go around was much better, and what I wanted to remember as that very special milestone.

"This was where our love story began," he announced, his eyes soft with affection, an elated smile parting those beautiful lips. He gripped my hands and rubbed his fingers over my knuckles. "And I hope it's also where our *forever* begins." He released my right hand and dropped to his knee, reaching into his pocket.

My hand shot to my mouth, covering a gasp. *Is he about to...?*

"Taylor Marie Wesley, I spent far too many years trying to keep from loving you. I wasted so much time... time that we could've been happy together. I won't waste any more. Will you do me the honor of becoming my wife?" He released my hand and opened a black velvet box. I didn't even look at the ring. I fell on my knees in front of him and pulled his face to mine, planting my lips on his.

"Yes!" I cried between kisses. "Yes," I repeated, hoping this wasn't a dream. If it was, I never wanted to wake up.

We kissed for what seemed like forever before I finally pulled away, my eyes damp with happy tears.

"Do you want the ring now?"

"Oh, the ring!" I'd been so overjoyed with the prospect of becoming his wife, I forgot all about the ring. "Yes. Give it to me." His laughter filled the air once more and my face heated. I didn't mean to be that blunt and demanding, but I wanted it more than I'd ever wanted any material thing in my life. My breath stuck in my throat when he finally aimed the open box in my direction.

"Dalton," I breathed, my eyes flashing to his. It was perfect. A vintage halo diamond ring with a rose gold band. I couldn't have designed a more fitting ring myself. He slid it out of the black velvet cushion and grabbed my left hand.

"I can't wait to spend the rest of my life fighting with you so we can have incredible make up sex." A giggle erupted from my lips as he slid the cool band onto my ring finger.

"Let's start right now," I offered. He wrapped me in his arms and our lips met with the same electric intensity as they had the first time we kissed on this beach. The sky darkened as we rushed toward our bungalow, where he made love to me for the first time as the future Mrs. Dalton James. We forgot all about the fight, but we sure remembered how to make up.

The End

Acknowledgements

There are so many people I want to thank, but I'll try to make this brief. First and foremost, I want to thank you, the reader for giving Six Nights in Paradise a chance. I'm so glad I was able to publish this book when I did considering it was originally slated for fall. With everything going on in the world today, this book is the escape many of us need right now.

To my husband, thank you for listening to my ramblings about these characters and entertaining our boys so I can sneak away and get a few words in even when our lives are beyond hectic.

To my alpha readers, Bobbie-Jo & Tricia, thank you for all your support and encouragement. You two have always been in my corner cheering me on. I probably never would have pursued this dream if it hadn't been for you guys telling me to just keep writing.

Thank you to my awesome betas, Jennifer, Brittany, Amanda, Katelyn, and Tiffany who took the time to read the first draft and help me (hopefully) perfect the finished product.

To my editor, Stacy, you are a miracle worker! I'm so grateful you were able to squeeze me in to your already packed schedule so I could release this book earlier than originally planned. Also, thank you for once again working your magic on my manuscript and polishing my words. They always look much better after you've gotten ahold of them.

Thank you J.M. Walker/Just Write Creations for formatting this beauty for me! It's been a pleasure to work with you.

To my cover designer, and all around bad ass, Cassy Roop, thank you for creating another beautiful cover for me! Your talent never ceases to amaze me.

Thank you, Tiffany for all that you do! From being my sounding board to reading 75 versions of the same blurb until

I get it right (lol), you are always there when I need you. I could not ask for a better PA. Thank you for also proofreading this book on extremely short notice and tolerating my fly-by-the-seat-of-my-pants approach to everything.

To the incredible teams at Wildfire Marketing and Enticing Journey, thank you for all your hard work and helping me bring Taylor & Dalton's story to so many new readers.

Last, but not least, I thank God for every blessing in my life.

About the Author

Ashley is an author and book lover living in Ohio with her husband and two sons. She's loved reading since childhood and has always enjoyed creating characters and stories. She finds inspiration everywhere: a song on the radio, a person she passes on the street, a place she's visited on vacation. She lets her imagination run wild and her fingers do the typing.

Connect with Ashley
Newsletter - eepurl.com/gdWc9H
Facebook - facebook.com/authorashleycade
Twitter - twitter.com/AuthorAshCade
Instagram - instagram.com/authorashleycade

Goodreads -
goodreads.com/author/show/18600951.Ashley_Cade
Bookbub - bookbub.com/authors/ashley-cade
Pinterest - pinterest.com/authorashleycade
Website - authorashleycade.com/

Made in the USA
Monee, IL
04 April 2021